SPY IN SPACE

This Armada book belongs to:

_____

_____

_____

Patrick Moore read his first book on astronomy when he was six, and is now a world-wide authority on the subject. He is Director of the British Astronomical Association Lunar Section, was awarded the OBE in 1968, and is well-known as a television and radio personality—he has presented the BBC television programme "The Sky at Night" for the last twenty years.

He is the author of a variety of books for both adults and children, and his hobbies include cricket, music and chess.

Also available in Armada by Patrick Moore

Scott Saunders Space Adventure Series
PLANET OF FEAR

More "Scott Saunders" adventures will be published in Armada

Patrick Moore

SPY IN SPACE

A Scott Saunders Space Adventure

An Original Armada

Spy In Space was first published in the UK in Armada in 1977
by Fontana Paperbacks, 14 St. James's Place, London SW1A 1PF

© Patrick Moore 1977

Printed in Great Britain by
Love & Malcomson Ltd., Brighton Road,
Redhill, Surrey.

CONTENTS

CHAPTER 1

ALPHA

The great space station glittered in the sunlight. It was oddly-shaped, and not in the least like one of the graceful "space wheels" to be found in books written before the first astronauts flew. One radio commentator had even described it as being like a hairbrush, with teeth sticking out from the main cigar-shaped body. Yet it was one of Man's greatest achievements of the twentieth century, and as the ferry-rocket drew up to the Station Scott Saunders stared at it with wonder and respect.

He turned to the only other occupant of the ferry. "I never thought it would look quite like this, sir. You're used to it, but it's different for me!"

Ashley Fenton gave him a friendly grin. "Well, I've done two tours of duty here, and one on the American station, so I reckon I'm starting to think of space as 'home'. How are you feeling? You don't seem to be worried by zero gravity, at least."

"I'm enjoying it," said Scott truthfully. "I can't wait to go on board—if that's what you call it. I only hope they don't take one look at me and send me back on the next ferry."

Fenton eyed him critically. Scott was fair-haired, blue-eyed and stocky; somehow he seemed different from most of the teenage cadets who came to the Station, if only because he looked younger. "How old are you? Fifteen?"

"Sixteen," said Scott, a little indignantly. "Don't I look it?"

"Hardly. Not that it matters; you won the scholarship, and if you can make the grade during the next couple of weeks you ought to be taken on as a full-time trainee. Get ready, kid. We're going to dock."

Scott settled down on his couch, and watched closely as the pilot operated the controls. He had been in space for only an hour, and never before had he known what it would feel like to be weightless; before the flight he had been half-afraid of feeling sick, but even during blast-off from Woomera Base he had been too excited to worry. As the ferry drifted closer and closer to the Station, the minutes seemed to drag. Scott remembered what he had been told by Commander Thomson, who had been in charge of the Station for many years now: "Don't forget, boy—space is hostile. Make no mistake about that. Act sensibly, and treat it with respect." Now, at last, the great moment was near.

Suddenly Fenton gave an impatient exclamation, and there was a brief burst of power from the motors; the ferry shuddered slightly, and Scott looked up. "Anything wrong, sir."

"Not sure yet. Don't talk," said Fenton shortly, and Scott waited. Again the motors came into action, only to stop once more. Through the window the Station was outlined against the blackness of the sky, but it was further away now, and Fenton spoke into the microphone. "Ferry to Station One. Do you read me? Over."

There was a pause. Scott could not hear the reply, but after a few moments Fenton spoke again. "Understood. Docking mechanism faulty. I have a scholar-

8

ship boy with me. May I have permission to come across in suits? Over."

He turned up the controls, and this time Scott could hear a voice which he recognized as Commander Thomson's. He had never actually met the head of the Station, but he had spoken to him on television before he had begun the flight, so that he knew what to expect. "No reason why not, but make sure the boy knows what he has to do. Decision is yours."

Fenton turned his head. "No need to get worried, kid, but as you've probably gathered the docking mechanism has developed a fault. We can put it right easily enough, but it'll take a bit of time. We'll have to do a space-walk. Nervous?"

"Of course not. I'm hardly a kid," said Scott, and Fenton chuckled. "Ready when you are."

"Right. Get your suit on, and I'll give you a run-down on how to work it. I'll have to stay on the ferry, but you won't be on your own for more than a few hundred yards."

It was only then that Scott realized that he would have nobody with him, and for a moment he felt his heart thumping, but he did his best not to show any surprise. "I don't mind—but you'd better tell me just where I'm to go!"

Fenton nodded, and pointed through the observation window. "See that section there?—if you look, you can make out the docking port where we ought to have gone in. Make straight for it, and you'll be met. Incidentally," he added, "you can't float away, because you'll have a lifeline with you, and it'll stay firmly fixed on the ferry until you're safely inside the Station port. Hurry up. Suit on, and I'll check it through with you."

Scott obeyed. He was honest enough to admit to

9

himself that he was scared; being alone in space during his first trip was quite enough to unnerve any sixteen-year-old, but he had no intention of showing his feelings. In any case, he had been well taught back on Earth, and he knew about the various working parts of the spacesuit, notably the miniature rocket booster which gave him enough thrust to carry him along at a reasonable speed. It was a full twenty minutes before Fenton was satisfied, and Scott gave a final look round the cramped cabin of the ferry. "Ready, sir."

Fenton gave him a hard look. "Are you sure? If you've any doubts at all, now is the time to say so."

"I said I'm ready," repeated Scott, hoping that his voice sounded firm. "Look, sir, I've waited a long time for this!"

"Good lad. On your way, then," said Fenton. "Get inside the airlock, and wait for me to reduce pressure. Let me know as soon as the indicator reads zero, and then open the door and step out."

It was only when he was inside the airlock, with a solid door between him and Fenton, that Scott started to feel genuinely scared. He knew that there was no chance of falling; he and the ferry were both whirling round the Earth at a dizzy speed, but there was no sensation of movement, and he remembered what one of his school teachers had told him: "Picture two ants on a bicycle-wheel. Spin the wheel, and the ants won't fly apart, because they're travelling in the same direction at the same rate. In the same way, a space-walker won't fly away from his rocket." All the same, it was a frightening prospect.

He watched the indicator, and saw the needle swinging steadily from 'normal air pressure' to 'zero'. Then he heard Fenton's voice in the earphones of his helmet. "On your way, kid."

Scott breathed hard, and pushed against the outer door. It swung open, and for the first time in his life he faced the black emptiness of space. All round him, so it seemed, there were stars—except in one direction, where the huge bulk of Station One hid the glare of the sun. Then he looked below, and saw the coloured, far-away Earth, looking more like a giant map than a globe; after all, he was 'only' five hundred miles up. For a moment he felt sick, and he wondered whether everyone had been wrong. Once he stepped out of the airlock, it seemed only too likely that he would fall down, down, down until he hit the ground.

"All right?" came Fenton's voice, and Scott swallowed hard. For an instant he closed his eyes, and then pushed away from the ferry. Now he was 'floating', and he gave a quick tug at the life-line which fastened him to the body of the rocket.

"No need to use your booster," said Fenton casually. "If you did as you were told, you'll have given yourself enough momentum to glide across. I've told them you're on your way."

In fact the distance between the ferry and the docking port of Station One was greater than Scott had expected; as he learned in after years, judging distances in space was never an easy matter. Steadily he glided across, and the Station loomed larger and larger. Then he saw something else. A spacesuited figure had appeared from the far side, but there was no lifeline, and he heard a new voice in his headphones. "Can't use my——" The words were blurred. "Drifting. Get me——"

Fenton cut in. "Emergency. Ferry to Station. Emergency! Will attempt rescue——"

Scott spun himself round, using a brief thrust from

11

his tiny rocket motor. Again he heard a blurred cry, and he called out. "I've seen him, sir. I'll unlock and go after him——"

"Don't be a young fool," roared Fenton. "You can't do it. Wait, and I'll be out. Stay where you are!"

Scott thought furiously. "No time. He's drifting fast—I'll have to get him." He operated the switch which released his lifeline, and then felt for the main booster. "Nothing else for it!"

Fenton's voice came through again, but Scott was not listening; his eyes were fixed on the drifting figure, now spinning over and over and moving further away every second. He pressed the thrust control, and shot forward, but for a moment he lost his bearings, and he too started to spin round. Desperately he struggled with the controls, and managed to right himself, but learning about 'space-walking' in the comfort of a classroom was very different from the real thing, and he felt a surge of panic. Then he heard Fenton, this time speaking slowly and calmly. "All right, kid. Keep your head. Give counter-thrust, and take it easy. I'll be with you as soon as I can."

Luckily Scott had made the best use of his time at training school—otherwise, as he thought even at that moment, he would not be where he was. After what seemed an age he had his movements under control, but by now the drifting figure had dwindled almost to a speck, and seemed to have stopped struggling. Scott applied the full power of his booster, and knew that he was moving quickly, even though the only way he could tell was by seeing how fast the ferry-rocket seemed to shrink. "I can see him. I reckon I can get to him——"

Again he almost started to spin, but by now he was becoming used to the controls, and to his relief

12

he saw that he was racing up to the unknown astronaut. At the critical moment he applied reverse thrust, and almost before he realized it he was within arm's-length of his target. "Can you hear me?" he said, as calmly as he could. "If so, grab my suit."

"Oxygen—no good," came a gasping voice, and Scott tensed. "Must have air—quick!"

With a final thrust Scott moved across, and his suit cannoned against the astronaut's body. Before he could begin to drift away again Scott grabbed, and the two spun round together. Training stood Scott in good stead. In a matter of seconds he had fastened his spare lead on to the other man's suit, and fumbled with the controls of his reserve oxygen tank. "I'm going to connect you to my spare," he said rapidly. "Keep still, or you'll finish us both."

Working under such conditions would have been difficult even for a trained astronaut, and Scott was hardly that, but somehow or other he fixed the lead into place, and waited. "Oxygen coming in. Can you hear me?"

A gasp. "Yes—that's—that's done it. I can't use my motor—out of action. Hang on to me if you can!"

"I've got you," said Scott, and did his best to look round. They were a terrifying distance from the Station now, and he wondered dismally whether his booster had enough power left to bring them back, even if he could judge the distance correctly. "Don't try to help me. I guess I can manage."

He operated the control, and with agonizing slowness the two began to move, but not in the right direction, and Scott realized that they were still far from safety. He could hear his companion's heavy, jerky breathing, but little else, and again he gave a brief burst of power. "Scott Saunders to Station One.

13

Saunders to Station One. Do you read me? Over!"

"Station One to Saunders. Hold tight. We're coming!"

Scott could not make out whether the voice was Fenton's, but he gave a cry of relief, and relaxed; surely all he had to do now was wait? Then he took a grip on himself. "I've pulled it off so far, and I'd better try to finish it," he thought, and risked another burst. This time his judgement was better, and the Station seemed to shoot toward him. Then he saw that he was no longer alone; there were several space-suited figures near him, and he called again. "Saunders to Station. I'm coming in."

"Take it easy," came the reply, and this time the voice was unmistakably Fenton's. "Make for the dock. Give reverse thrust in ten seconds."

Scott obeyed. Almost before he realized it he was gliding up to the Station, and he felt a lifeline fall across him; he relaxed, and then, suddenly, reaction set in. A red mist swirled in front of his eyes, and he lost consciousness.

"He's coming round," said a voice, and Scott opened his eyes, blinking stupidly around him. "That was close! I don't reckon he'll ever be much closer to death than he was then. All right, Scott?"

Scott sat up, and spluttered. "I—yes, I'm fine. Did I get him?"

"You did indeed. That was as brave an action as I've seen in years. Drink this."

Scott took the container, and squirted some liquid down his throat; ordinary drinking was impossible in a space station, where everything was weightless. His head cleared, and he looked round. There were five other men in the cabin—or, rather, four men and a boy; one of the five looked no older than Scott

14

himself, while another was recognizable at once as Richard Thomson, commander of Station One. "Sorry I passed out. I couldn't help it."

"I'm only surprised that you didn't pass out a good deal earlier," said Thomson grimly. "I think we owe you an explanation, Scott." Dazed as he was, Scott could not help noticing the use of his Christian name rather than the formal 'Saunders'. "First, you'd better meet the young man you rescued—Nigel Lorrimer. Say 'thank you' nicely Nigel!"

"What can I say?" The boy shrugged, and looked embarrassed; his face was chalk-white, and he was shaking. "If you hadn't plugged in that oxygen lead when you did, I'd have been done for. My tank was empty, and there was no time for anyone else to reach me. I—well, I won't forget it."

"I will," said Scott, and managed a grin. He could think clearly now, and somehow he felt that he was among real friends. "It was sheer luck; I didn't really know what I was doing. I thought I was going to overshoot you by miles."

"You nearly did," said Thomson dryly. "It was a nasty moment, as you'll know only too well. You'd better meet the rest of us before I try to put you in the picture. Sir Eustace Wainwright—you've probably heard of him. Incidentally, Nigel is his nephew. Ashley Fenton you know, needless to say. And last, if not least, Dr. Reginald Fordyce Vale, who prefers to be called 'Reggie' rather than 'Scruff'. How do you feel?"

"On top of the world—literally," said Scott, and eased himself to his feet; by now he was becoming used to moving around under conditions of zero gravity. "I reckon I'm darned glad to be here!"

He looked quickly round at the two strangers. Sir

Eustace was short and rather plump; the most notice-able thing about him was a huge moustache which made him look rather like an amiable walrus. Vale was quite different. He was tall and lean, and wildly untidy; his spectacles were fastened to his ears by a piece of string, and his collar was askew, while his pockets bulged with an assortment of odds and ends. Sir Eustace held out his hand formally. "Welcome to our happy home," he said. "Rather an unusual entrance, if I may say so, but not an unpromising one. You agree, Reggie?"

"What do you think?' Vale broke into a laugh. "I think we owe our young friend a full explanation, even though things didn't go quite as we'd planned."

"No," murmured Sir Eustace. "They didn't, did they? Let me assure you, my dear Scott, that we had no intention of sending you out into space like some wandering comet. Naturally, we thought that every-thing was tied up in every sense of the term."

Scott looked puzzled. "I don't get it, sir. What do you mean?"

"Quite simple," said Thomson. "First, you don't really imagine that we'd let a raw cadet go space-walking on his own without keeping a very careful check on him? As you know, we have a good many young men up here, and what we try to do is to sort them out. The docking fault was, of course, rubbish; we could have docked the ferry quite normally if we'd wanted to, but as a matter of principle we make all our candidates 'walk the plank' to see whether they can keep their nerve. You passed that test all right, but—well, there were some things we hadn't bargained for."

Scott blinked. "But—you don't mean that the whole thing was a put-up job?"

"Of course it wasn't," said Vale impatiently. "Use your intelligence. Actually I think I was the man they were after, not Nigel, but the result was the same."

Sir Eustace waved his hand. "Don't fog the issue, Scruff."

"I'm not fogging anything—and if you call me 'Scruff' again I shall hit you with the nearest blunt instrument I can find. Confound you, I won't have it!"

For a moment Scott wondered whether Vale would turn out to be ill-tempered, but then he saw that both he and Sir Eustace were grinning, and Vale broke into a laugh. "Well, what about it? We've got to make up our minds about this lad, and we can't afford to make any mistakes. It's now or never."

Thomson nodded. "I agree," he said quietly. "Well, Eustace, do we tell him the whole story?"

Sir Eustace paused, and then nodded back. "Yes. Go on."

"Right. Listen, Scott. The space-walk was part of the trial we give to all youngsters who come here, but the rest of the business wasn't. Nigel was genuinely in danger—in fact, in as tricky a position as anyone could be; and it wasn't an accident. There's no doubt in my mind that it was a deliberate attempt at murder."

Scott stared. "You can't be serious!"

"I was never more serious in my life," said Thomson calmly. "We are dealing with a collection of highly sinister gentlemen who belong to an organization which we've nicknamed 'Alpha' for want of anything better—and unless we can smash them, the results, not only for the Station, but for the whole of civilization, may be very nasty indeed."

CHAPTER 2

THE MYSTERIOUS SPACE STATION

There was a long silence. Scott's brain was in a whirl; this was the last sort of situation he had expected to find, and for a moment he wondered whether he could be the victim of an elaborate practical joke. But Thomson's face was set and grim, and even Sir Eustace had a deadly serious expression.

"How many people know about this, sir?" asked Scott at last.

Thomson shrugged. "That's something I can't tell you—and neither can the rest of us. If we knew, we'd all be a great deal happier. But there is one point which worries me above all else. There aren't many people on this Station, and everyone has been very carefully checked by Intelligence. None the less, one of us—and it may be anyone—is a member of Alpha."

"We've got to face it," said Vale, producing a battered pipe from his threadbare jacket and cramming it with tobacco—not an easy task under conditions of weightlessness. "I was due to go out to do some routine checks a couple of hours ago, but at the last moment something cropped up, and Nigel went instead. When he was through the airlock, his suit failed. The rocket booster had been damaged, and the oxygen tank was empty. It can't have been an accident, because the dials had been altered so that nothing looked out of

18

order. If you hadn't come on the scene, we would have been one short by now."

"If——" began Scott.

"Don't interrupt, confound you. I may say that it isn't the first time there has been an attempt to rub me out, so evidently the people behind Alpha have me marked down." Vale snorted. "If I get my hands on them, I'll see what I can remember of the karate I learned at school. That was a long time ago now, but I haven't forgotten it all."

"I'd feel almost sorry for the blighters," murmured Sir Eustace. "Don't be under any false impressions, Scott my boy. Scruff may look like a demented scarecrow, but I'm not flattering him when I say that when it comes to scientific gadgets and know-how he is very much the cat's whiskers, and Alpha doesn't like him one little bit."

Scott looked round helplessly. "But—what's their game, sir? And come to think of it, why are you telling me all this? I should think it's pretty hush-hush."

"Quite so," said Sir Eustace. "Generally speaking, the fewer the people who know about Alpha the better, if ony because we have no idea who is mixed up in it. As for their game—well, that's something else which beats us, but it looks as though they're trying to grab all the secret information they can, for reasons which are undoubtedly both deep and dirty. Which brings me on to the reason why we're talking so openly; that happens to be my own particular department. I may be both old and dim-witted, but I'm still officially head of Intelligence, and I have a habit of making snap decisions."

"Head of Intelligence, sir?"

Sir Eustace bowed. "Amazingly, yes. I don't go

about advertising the fact, of course—and if you have any ideas about my moustache being false, you can forget them. It's genuine enough, and if you doubt me you have my full permission to try to pull it off. False beards and face-fungus went out fifty years ago."

Scott looked at Sir Eustace with a new respect. Anyone less like an Intelligence chief could scarcely have been pictured. "That's all very well, sir, but where do I come in?"

"If you'll wait for just a moment and let me marshal my thoughts, such as they are, I'll tell you." Sir Eustace paused. "Up here, on Station One—or the European Station, or whatever you call it—we are, obviously, doing a great deal of work. As you probably remember from school, the first permanent Station went up in 1985, which is more than ten years ago now, and as time goes by these orbiting bases will become more and more important, not only because they're observation platforms and research laboratories but also because they are our vital links with the Moon. Things go on here which we don't broadcast to the world at large. You follow me so far?"

Scott nodded.

"Splendid. Well, the future of science—and everything else—depends on Youth, with a capital Y. Therefore, our policy is to recruit people whom we can really trust and train them up. You came here because you won a scholarship, but frankly we've been watching you carefully for some time now, and I believe you'll make the grade."

Scott felt bewildered. "There must be plenty of others, sir!"

"Not so many as you might think. Most of our teenagers come here, spend a few weeks on the Station,

20

and then go on to follow very useful and highly respectable careers. Two of them have gone a stage further, and you'll meet them shortly; one is English, by name Alec Kerry, and the other is, of all things, an Icelander named Thor Eiriksson. But even so, I'm not one hundred per cent sure of them yet."

Vale puffed at his pipe, producing a cloud of black smoke that billowed across the cabin. "Neither am I, and you know it."

"Quite so. But while you were lying on your back, young Scott, we had a brief discussion, and we're taking a gamble on you. Correct, my dear Richard?"

Thomson nodded.

"Let me ask you one thing," went on Sir Eustace, still in the same casual tone. "Will you promise me, without the shadow of a doubt, that nothing of what you learn here will go beyond the team in which you'll be working?"

"Of course I promise, sir. I can't take it in yet," said Scott haltingly. "After all, it's only a couple of hours since I left Earth—"

Sir Eustace leaned forward, and his bantering manner dropped from him like a cloak. "Very well, then. I needn't tell you that things are much too serious for us to run the slightest risk. Whatever you are asked to do, or whatever danger you may run, you must follow orders. Old-fashioned loyalty may be rare nowadays, but it's something we've got to have. If you can't give us that undertaking, I'll send you home on the next ferry. It's up to you."

Scott looked him squarely in the eye. "I understand, sir. I won't let you down."

"Good." Sir Eustace relaxed, and fingered his moustache. "In that case there are various things you'll have to know, quite apart from your normal duties,

21

and I suggest that we leave the first briefing to Nigel. You're sure you're happy about things?"

Scott hardly knew what to say, but he always remembered the next few moments. Thomson, Sir Eustace, Vale, Fenton and Nigel took turns in shaking his hand solemnly; it was rather like a school ceremony, but Scott realized that it would alter the whole course of his life. Then Sir Eustace beamed at him. "Well, having got that little piece of business over, you'd better see your quarters—you'll get very used to them after a time, and I promise that they'll grow on you. Shepherd him along, Nigel, there's a good chap. The rest of us had better go round and do some more checking. One useless spacesuit is bad enough, but there may be others, and I don't think any of us want a repeat performance of that remarkable drama just now."

The 'quarters', as Sir Eustace called them, were installed in the main hub of the Station. Nigel led the way, and Scott followed him rather clumsily; he was still getting used to the feeling of being weightless, and it was impossible to tell which was 'up' and which was 'down'. Yet the rooms themselves were surprisingly comfortable, and Scott began to feel very much at home. Then Nigel put his hand on Scott's shoulder. "Look, I haven't said much yet; I still feel a bit rocky. Why did you do it?"

"What?"

"Come after me, of course. I don't believe I'd have had the nerve." Nigel stopped short. "Sorry; I didn't mean to embarrass you, but we'll be together a lot from now on, and we'd better get to know each other."

"Suits me," said Scott. He liked the look of Nigel; also, it was good to be with someone of his own age. "How old are you?"

"Seventeen—just. I feel a bit of a fraud, because if I wasn't the nephew of the Head of Intelligence I suppose I wouldn't be here. What do you think of my uncle, by the way?"

"I—well, I was fooled by him at first," said Scott slowly. "He must be pretty brainy."

"That's putting it mildly. He enjoys making himself out to be an ass," said Nigel, and grinned. "We've got quite a team up here. Reggie Vale is probably the most brilliant scientist in the world, and there's nobody who knows more about rockets than Ashley Fenton does. Then, of course, there's Commander Thomson. He's been here for ten years now."

"Ten years?" repeated Scott. "Phew! that's some time!"

"He'll never go down," said Nigel quietly. "He can't. Do you realize that he hasn't any legs?"

Scott stared. "You must be joking!"

"I'm not. When he first came up here there was a ghastly accident. I wasn't around then, of course; I was still at prep school, but I heard all about it. Richard Thomson had both his legs sliced off, and it was touch and go whether he'd pull through at all. So long as he's weightless he's as active as you and me, and his tin legs don't notice, but if he went down to Earth he'd be a cripple—and I can't imagine he'd like that!"

"Not much," muttered Scott. "He must feel pretty bad about it."

"I don't think so. He hasn't any family, and he once told me that space is his home—which makes sense all right. Come to think of it, how about you? You've no family either."

Scott looked surprised. "How did you know?"

"Because I'm one of the team, and you were checked

23

over before you came," said Nigel simply. "Sorry if I stirred things up."

Scott shrugged. "Oh, I'm not worried about it. I haven't the slightest idea who my parents were, and I was brought up in an orphanage, so I've no relations —but I've never had any, so I don't miss them. Friends are what matter."

"I wouldn't be surprised if we hit it off, pal," said Nigel, and grinned. "That's how it seems to me, quite apart from your hooking me up like a stranded fish. Strange how things work out, isn't it? The other two 'youngsters', as Uncle Eustace calls them, haven't quite fitted into the picture yet."

"Who are they, then?"

"Alec Kerry and Thor Eiriksson. They're over in the American Station at the moment," said Nigel. "They've been doing the grand tour, and that's something you'll have to do as well pretty soon. Alec's the same age as me. I knew him back at Woomera, and we trained together. Thor may be a bit older, but not much. I'm sure he's got Viking blood in him!"

Scott lay back, floating freely above the floor of the cabin. "What do you mean by the grand tour? Going round the other Stations?"

"That's it. I'd better put you in the picture," said Nigel. "We call ourselves No. 1, though our proper title is the European Station. Apart from the people you've met, the permanent residents—as they call themselves—are Juan Santos from Spain, Milo Rigetti from Italy, a Greek named Constantine Londos, and dear old Peter Monk, who wouldn't go home to Earth if you paid him a fortune; he's much too interested in his cosmic rays and sunspots. Maintenance crews

24

change every few months, and at the moment we've got a visitor from Lenin Station as well."

"That's the Russian one, I suppose?"

"Correct. Gregory Voronov is the man over here; he's a decent type, and his English is pretty good. Over on Lenin there must be a couple of dozen Russkies, and they generally keep rather to themselves, though they're pleasant enough when we want to go across. The American Station is more fun; we call it the Cape Canaveral Hotel, because they seem to have parties all the time! Clyde Warren and Hamilton Fisher are the two Yanks we know best, and they're here quite often."

"Sounds great," said Scott. "That makes three. What about Station Four? It's a research base, if what we were told back home is true."

"Ye—es," said Nigel slowly. "It's much smaller than the others, and there are only three permanent scientists there—a Japanese, Professor Nagata; a Frenchman named Dupont, and Carl Brand, who comes from somewhere in Central Europe. It's not far away at the moment, and it's moving in the same orbit as we are. Want to have a look at it?"

Scott nodded. "Rather."

"Easy enough," said Nigel, and swung himself over to the cabin wall. He slid back a steel panel, disclosing a transparent window; then he turned out the lights, plunging the tiny compartment into darkness. The sun was on the far side of the Station, so that Scott could see the stars shining from the inky blackness of the sky, and there was something else too; a brilliant point which shifted very slowly against the starry background. "Is that it?"

"That's Station Four," said Nigel. "Take a good look at it, pal. Seems innocent enough, and yet I've a

25

hunch that it is by no means quite what it ought to be."

"What do you mean? Are you thinking of—what do you call it—Alpha?"

Nigel nodded, his expression grim and set. "I am. There's no proof, and even my uncle thinks I'm crazy, but—well, I can't help it. If we're going to track these brutes down, I believe we'll have to start by finding out as much as we can about Station Four. It won't be easy, but it'll have to be done."

CHAPTER 3

EMERGENCY!

During the next few weeks Scott learned to know every square inch of Station One. It was a strange place, but in a surprisingly short time he came to regard it as his true home, and he had not the slightest wish to go back to Earth. It was easy to understand how Commander Thomson felt.

Nigel was his constant companion, and though they said nothing outwardly, both boys knew that they had formed a link which nothing could break. It was several days before the other two cadets, Alec and Thor, came back from their trip to the American Station, both in high spirits and obviously ready to be friendly. Alec Kerry was tall and dark, with a quick smile and a keen sense of humour; Thor Eiriksson looked the typical Viking, even though his English was almost perfect.

26

"You know," said Alec on one occasion, when the four boys were relaxing after they had been busy checking equipment, "we're lucky—all of us. I know the Station has been here for more than ten years, but we're in almost at the beginning, and we're having a great time as well as doing a useful job. If we'd stayed 'down there', I suppose we'd have been sitting in some stuffy office all day—or fishing for cod off Iceland!"

Thor chuckled. "You can keep your cod, my friend. But if you like, I'll take you for a sail next time we go down."

"That'll be some time." Alec burst into song. "A spaceman's life for me——"

Nigel hurled a book at him, and there was a general scuffle; but Scott did not forget the remark. He was indeed lucky. If he had not won that scholarship his life would have followed a different course, and he was determined to make the most of the chance that he had been given. He knew, too, that both Commander Thomson and Sir Eustace were watching him carefully to see how he shaped, and now and again he was summoned to conferences which included Nigel but not either Alec or Thor.

Pleasant though it was, life on the Station was very far from idle. Each scientist was carrying out some particular research programme, and Scott soon came to know at least a little of what was being done. Londos, the Greek doctor, was busy on medical work; as he explained, there were various operations and experiments which could be carried out only under zero gravity, and several times Scott acted as assistant. Milo Rigetti was the communications expert, and spent much of his time in the radio arm of the Station, while the quiet, scholarly Peter Monk and

27

the ever-cheerful, Juan Santos were fanatical astronomers. There were frequent visits from both the Russians and the Americans, and Scott realized that all the space-men were of the same general type. Race, language and creed meant nothing to an astronaut.

Vale's position was less clear-cut, and at first he was not inclined to say a great deal about what he was doing. Finally Scott plucked up enough courage to ask him outright. They were on their own; Ashley Fenton was across in the Russian Station, and Nigel was resting after a spell of duty when Scott joined Vale in the radio room. "Do you mind if I ask you some questions, sir?"

Vale took out his pipe, crammed it with tobacco and lit up, producing the usual cloud of evil-smelling smoke. "I don't in the least mind being asked questions, but when we're alone I have the strongest objections to being called 'sir'. If you use that ridiculous nickname I shall undoubtedly tip you overboard, so you'd better refer to me as Reggie. What's on your mind?"

"You," said Scott bluntly. "Look, if I'm going to be of any use I'll have to know just what's going on, and I don't believe I've got the full story yet."

Vale grinned, and took off his spectacles, polishing them absent-mindedly on a piece of oily rag. "I was wondering when you'd come to the point. You're right, of course. If you want to know the truth—well, it's my job to see that nobody takes a pot-shot at us. You may think that everything in space is nice and friendly, but it isn't—not by a long chalk. I'm spending my time in developing an electric screen which will make us immune to attack, whatever form it may take."

28

Scott looked puzzled. "What kind of a screen?"

"If I wanted to give you all the details I'd have to begin by giving you a course in electronics that takes most people years, but I'll do my best." Vale replaced his spectacles on his nose, and settled himself down in the manner of a schoolmaster. "Generally speaking, any attack on a Station has to be a physical one—I don't mean anything so antique as a bomb, though I suppose that would do; I'm thinking of a guided missile, and goodness knows there are plenty of military warheads stockpiled in Pekin, Moscow, Washington, and, for that matter, London. There hasn't been a major war for a long time, but it could come, and without protection any space station is a sitting duck waiting to be wiped out. There's Alpha to be borne in mind, as well. The best way to deal with a nuclear missile is to make it destroy itself before it can get close enough to do any damage. Hence my screen, which you won't be able to see or feel, but which ought to be a great deal more effective than any armour-plating."

"It's a new idea, then?"

"Quite new. I modestly claim that I thought it out myself, even though I can't yet prove that it will work; I suppose it depends on whether I join up any wires the wrong way. In principle, I'm fitting transmitters in various positions around the Station and connecting them up to a generator which draws its power from the sun. These generators focus their energy at a set distance, and that's where the screen will be. Unless I'm on the wrong track, any missile will come to a sudden and violent end as soon as it hits the barrier."

Scott whistled. "I see. How many people know about it, sir—Reggie, I mean?"

"Not many. On this Station, the only people in the secret are Richard Thomson, Eustace, Ashley, Nigel and yourself. I don't think I need tell you how deathly hush-hush it is. Our mysterious friends in Alpha may have some idea that I'm up to something, but I hope they don't know quite what."

"When will it be ready?"

"Fairly soon, with any luck at all. I've been working flat out, as you know, and I'm going to make my first real test in a few months, so be on the look-out. I think I've made my own personal cubby-holes safe against any prowlers, but one never knows. For your ear alone, I have my main bits and pieces in Cabin 36—and anyone who tries to break into it is due for a rather nasty shock."

Scott looked thoughtful. "But—well, there's nobody here on the Station whom you can't trust—"

"Use your brains," said Vale roughly. "Remember, Alpha is everywhere. Goodness knows who belongs to it and who doesn't. How can we tell that they haven't got one of their agents within a few yards of us right at this moment? All right; look round—Peter Monk, Milo Rigetti, Juan Santos—so far as we know, all one hundred per cent loyal, but I can't be sure."

"And yet you seem to be sure of me," muttered Scott.

Vale grinned. "That's Eustace's decision. He got where he is now—Head of Intelligence—by making snap decisions and sticking by them. To the best of my knowledge he's only been badly wrong once, which is a pretty good record, and you and Nigel happen to be his choices. I'm bound to say that I agree with him, but that's by the by; I'm a scientist, not a head-shrinker. What about Thor and Alec?"

"I like them both," said Scott slowly; he could not

help being proud that Vale was treating him as an equal. "Thor's less easy to know, of course, because he's not English, but I reckon I'm starting to understand him. I think he's the first Icelander I've met."

"There aren't too many of them around. I like them, but I'm one of the few people who can chatter away in Icelandic, so I suppose I'm biased," said Vale. "Languages interest me, and it was worth while learning Icelandic simply to read the old Sagas! One day, when I've got time—What was that?"

Scott jumped up, forgetting for a moment that he was weightless. A sharp cracking noise echoed through the cabin, and then came a howling that he had heard only twice before, during alarm practises. "Emergency," said Vale briefly as the siren died away. "Spacesuit on, just in case!"

He lurched as a second cracking noise sounded from outside. Then, suddenly, there came a violent explosion, and the lights went out. The Station was no longer steady; it was shuddering, and Scott felt a wave of panic. "Suits on," roared Vale, and pulled back the shutter of the cabin window, so that light from the sun could flood in. Scott pulled himself together. Quickly he made for the cupboard which contained the spare vacuum equipment; each cabin was provided with two reserve suits—one of the safety-measures which Thomson had introduced early on in the Station's career.

Again the cabin lurched, and Scott cannoned into Vale, sending them both spinning against the far wall. The light faded as the sun passed out of view of the window, but there was still a little left, and in a few seconds both Scott and Vale had their suits in position.

"Don't start using oxygen yet," panted Vale. "We may need all we can save. Follow me!"

He switched on his portable flashlamp, and swung himself out of the door into the main corridor. Scott followed obediently, trying to clear his brain; was it an accident, or something worse? There seemed to be nobody else in the corridor, and he realized that Vale was heading away from the main control room. "Which way?"

"Don't ask questions. Just follow, and don't switch on your suit radio," breathed Vale. "Head for Cabin 36, and watch out!"

It was pitch-dark in the corridor, except for the pale beam from Vale's flashlamp, and Scott blundered along. Even though he had been on the Station for some weeks he was still not so agile as the really experienced astronauts, and moreover the Station was vibrating in a way that he had never known before. Suddenly Vale pulled up. "There's someone there. Take it easy!"

By now they had reached the junction of the third arm of the Station. It led away from the main corridor, and Vale's laboratory was at the far end of it, as Scott knew. The Station was still quivering, and then came a second signal; a wavering, high-pitched siren that could mean only one thing. "Oxygen on. We've been holed somewhere," rapped Vale, and Scott thrust the helmet down over his head, connecting up the leads and breathing deeply. Evidently there was serious damage, and he was desperately anxious about Nigel and the others.

Vale edged forward, switching off his torch; there was barely a glimmer of light, and Scott squinted through his transparent eyeshield. Then, without warning, Vale switched his torch on again, and Scott saw that the door of Cabin 36 was open. He saw too that there was a spacesuited figure inside, and Vale let out a roar. "Get him!"

The figure in the cabin straightened up, and swung his arm. Vale dodged, but not quickly enough; a metal case struck him on the head, and he let out a cry. Scott plunged forward, and met the intruder fairly and squarely. He grabbed, but too late; the unknown man was past him, and Scott dared not follow. He knew that the air-pressure was dropping alarmingly, and if Vale's suit had been damaged the danger was very real. Shining his torch, he forced himself down and peered through Vale's helmet. "Reggie. Are you all right?"

Vale choked. "I—yes, I'm all right. Who was it? Did you see him?"

"Not properly—there was no time. Where now?"

Vale managed to struggle up, and propelled himself across to the now-empty cabin. "Don't think he had time to do a lot. I wish I knew how he got in; the bang must have put all my alarms out of action. Back to Control, as quickly as you can." He pulled the door shut, and operated a concealed lock. "That won't be undone in a hurry. Get moving."

The lights came on again with startling suddenness, and Scott blinked in the glare, trying to make sense out of the jumble of voices in his earphones. Vale, still dazed and sick, swung back along the corridor, and Scott followed. "Nigel," he said softly into his microphone. "Nigel! What happened?"

Nigel's voice came through. "Darned great bang. In Arm One, we think. Nobody hurt, but it was a close call. Meet me in Control."

By the time Vale and Scott managed to reach the main nerve-centre of the Station the quaking had stopped, and the air-pressure was rising again; evidently the leak had been sealed off. Thomson and Sir Eustace were there, Thomson rapping out orders and Sir Eustace hovering in mid-air, surveying the scene with interest. "Well, Reggie? Anything to report?"

"Not much," said Vale shortly. "How bad is the damage?"

"Not too serious, fortunately. At least the pressure is back to normal; I never did like wearing these absurd suits." Sir Eustace lifted his helmet, and fingered his moustache. "Dear me!—that was quite a moment. With your permission, Richard, we'll have a roll-call and make sure that nobody has gone missing."

The Control Room was the largest cabin in the whole of the Station, and it contained all the main electronic equipment; Scott had as good a grasp of science as most people, but he had to admit that he knew very little about the banks of computers which lined the walls. There was a radar scanner in the centre of the room, and at the moment it was turned toward Earth; the outline of Australia showed up plainly, and Scott wondered whether the technicians at Woomera Rocket Base had the slightest idea of what was going on five hundred miles above their heads. By now most of the scientists had come in. Londos, Rigetti, Santos, Monk and both Thor and Alec were there, together with Gregory Voronov, the Russian astronomer who was a regular visitor. Scott felt Nigel's hand on his shoulder. "You had me worried, pal. Where were you? I couldn't get you on the buzzer——"

"Tell you later," whispered Scott, and then, aloud: "How about the observatory? Is it knocked around?"

Santos gave a grimace, but Peter Monk broke in;

he was one of the oldest men on the Station, with a face rather like that of a friendly parrot, and a quick, stuttering way of speaking. "It—it is a ruin. All our equipment broken. This is a disaster! If I had been in there myself, I would have been killed!"

"Listen to me, please," said Thomson loudly, and there was a sudden silence. "I'd better explain what has happened. There was a major explosion in the observatory, and it has affected part of Arm One, so that we've had to seal it off. I'll go outside and see the extent of the damage, and I'd like some help. Reggie, will you come?—Nigel—Alec—Thor. I'd be glad if the rest of you would go round the whole Station and make sure there's nothing else needing attention. Questions?'

Gregory Voronov swung forward. "Have you any idea of the cause, Commander? Could it have been deliberate?"

"I'll tell you that when we've had a close look. Keep your suits on for the time being, please. Hurry."

Vale pulled Scott aside. "Go back to my laboratory, and make sure that nobody else tries to get inside," he said softly. "I may be wrong, but I believe that there's a lot more to this than meets the eye. Stay on guard till I get back."

It was a full two hours before Vale returned. Scott waited patiently, but there were no further alarms, and at last he heard his name being called. "All right; Reggie here, and I'm on my way, so you can relax. We've fixed the leak. All systems are back to normal."

In a few minutes Vale appeared, together with Nigel. "Quite a business," said Vale grimly. "It might have been a great deal worse than it actually was. I take it you didn't see anyone?"

Scott shook his head. "Not a soul."

"It was a bomb, all right," muttered Nigel, white-faced and shaken. "Wish I could get my hands on the brute who planted it. It seems so pointless——"

"Not really," said Vale, and pointed to the cabin door. "I don't think I'm being conceited when I say that I was the indirect cause of it. The banger, whatever it may have been, was put in just the position to wreck all our alarms—not for long, but for several minutes. In fact, just long enough for our unknown friend to break into my laboratory and lay hands on the vital plans of my electric screen. If I hadn't realized what was happening, it would have worked."

Scott shook his head in bewilderment. "You must be right, I suppose, but—well, hang it all, it must have been one of us. Someone here, on the Station!"

"Exactly," said Vale. "I told you that Alpha was everywhere. If we hadn't been on guard, my bet is that by now the whole plan of my electronic screen would have been on its way to the people who are anxious to have it. And unless I'm out of my mind, some of those people at least are sitting comfortably inside Station Four."

CHAPTER 4

THE HIDDEN ENEMY

The next few days did a great deal to turn Scott into a hardened astronaut. The damage to the Station was worse than had been thought, as was painfully clear as soon as it could be examined from outside. Scott made countless 'space-walks', and he was busy upon repair work for all his waking time. The whole of the end of Arm One had been blown off; the observatory was a ruin, and the great telescope which Peter Monk and Juan Santos had been using was smashed beyond repair. Monk was persuaded to go down to Earth to make a report, leaving Santos to supervise the operations.

"Looks a mess," said Scott dismally, when he was outside with Nigel and Alec; by now he had learned how to control his pressure-suit, though he was always very careful to check it before going through the airlock, and he was never without a lifeline joining him to the Station itself. "Poor old Juan! he's broken-hearted."

"I don't wonder," said Alec, gliding up to the remains of the observatory wall. "It took goodness knows how many years to get all these bits and pieces working—and about ten seconds to blast them out of space. Alpha knows how to go about things."

Scott looked across at the faint speck of light which he knew to be Station Four, but he said nothing; Alec was not yet 'in the know', and neither for that matter was Thor, though to all outward appearances the four boys were on equal footing. Only on rare occasions did Sir Eustace call in Scott and Nigel for what he called 'a short chit-chat', overheard by nobody else apart from Thomson, Vale and sometimes Fenton.

It was at one of these confidential talks that Scott was given an insight into the full extent of the world space programme. For once Sir Eustace was not there, and neither was Vale; Thomson and Scott were alone, and Thomson seemed in a depressed mood. "I sometimes wish that I'd been born in another day and another place," he said wearily. "Human nature's a strange thing. We've achieved so much, and yet we seem to spend half our time in plotting against each other. It happens even up here."

"Alpha?" asked Scott thoughtfully.

"Of course. Oh, it would be so simple if we knew just who we were fighting," said Thomson; he sounded bitter, and quite unlike his usual self. "You've been here long enough to know your way around, and I'd value your opinions. Just what have you gathered about Alpha?"

Scott shrugged. "Precious little. When I first heard about it I thought it must be a bunch of terrorists, rather like the people who used to go about throwing bombs way back in the 1970s—but apparently it's more than that. It must be pretty well-run."

"It is," said Thomson. "In fact, the organization is quite brilliant. I'd better give you the facts—as far as I know them myself, which admittedly isn't far; remember, I've not been down on Earth for years, and I certainly won't go again." He glanced down at his legs, which looked so normal and which were no handicap to him on the Station, but which would leave him a cripple under conditions of 'ordinary' gravity. "There's no doubt that what Alpha wants is world domination, much as the Communists did until—luckily—they fought among themselves and split up. What I've never decided is whether the whole thing is run by a mad idealist, or by a power-crazy gang who want to set themselves up as dictators. Either way, it's dangerous."

A sudden thought came to Scott. "What about the United Nations people? Do they know about it?"

Thomson laughed. "Oh, they know about it—at least, they've been told—but you know as well as I do that the U.N. is as weak and useless as it was when it began. Also, I'm fairly sure that several of the key men in it are also key men in Alpha."

"That takes a bit of swallowing," muttered Scott.

"Possibly, but it's true enough. I've no cast-iron proof, but everything adds up," said Thomson. "Mind you, I doubt whether many of them know the full story. From what we've been able to find out, Alpha has a policy of dividing its activities up, so that nobody has enough knowledge to blow the whole thing sky-high."

"But——" Scott paused. "Well, there must be someone at the back of it all."

"Yes. And if it's someone who is a world figure, such as a highly-respected politician or even a leading scientist, he can do incalculable damage before he's finally tracked down. Alpha is everywhere, Scott—even here, as we've good reason to know after that little effort last month. How we got away without losing several lives I'll never know." Thomson looked up suddenly. "You've got to know Nigel and Ashley pretty well by now. What about Alec and Thor?"

"Decent guys," said Scott slowly. "They fit in all right . . . Look—why are you talking to me like this, rather than them? They've both been here for ages, and I'm a new boy!"

"I suppose you can call it instinct," said Thomson. "It's Eustace's decision, though I agree with it. Alec is a perfectly ordinary young man with a good background, good technical knowledge and good prospects, but whether he has the flair to make a real leader we don't yet know. Thor has a first-class brain, but he's just that bit too reserved so far. No; they're adequate —perhaps more—but Eustace felt that he wanted another trainee who would be on the same footing as

39

Nigel. You were the one he chose. I hope you feel suitably flattered," he added, with a sudden grin.

"I do," said Scott sincerely. "Is this where I say 'I'll play the game, sir!' and shake you by the hand?"

"I don't think you need bother. There is one thing you've not done yet, though, and that's to go across to the other two main Stations. Ashley is due for a flip across to Three—that's the Soviet base, as you know; they generally call it after dear old Lenin—and you'd better go along. Alec can go too."

Nothing could have suited Scott better. Gregory Voronov was a regular visitor to Station One, and so was Boris Kotov, the famous chemist; but as yet Scott had met none of the other Russians, and he welcomed the chance. Actually the trip did not take place, mainly because Ashley Fenton was so hard at work that he refused to be dragged away, but at last he was ready, and Vale called a conference. "I want you to go across in the big ferry," he said. "It's due to be tried out. I've been tinkering about with it, and I'll be glad to know how it behaves. Call up Three, and make sure they're ready for you."

By now Scott was thoroughly at home with the communications system, and it took him only a few minutes to establish contact. "All right to come over?" he said, as Voronov's face appeared on the television screen. "Ashley, Alec and me. Just a routine trip, I think."

"We will have the caviare and the vodka waiting," said Voronov seriously. "We will even lay out a red carpet. We will see you in an hour."

Station Three was an almost exact copy of Station One, and Scott felt very much at home as soon as he was inside. Out in space, nationality no longer seemed to matter; everyone was working for the same cause, and all the Russians were friendly and hospitable. Also, the system was much the same, and Voronov handed Scott and Alec over to the latest arrival—a young Soviet astronomer named Alexis Zayev, who was nineteen but looked much younger. His English was excellent, and he proved to be a first-class guide.

"I have heard of the trouble in your Base," he said after he had taken Scott and Alec on a tour of inspection. "What is the latest news?"

"It was pretty much of a mess," said Alec soberly. "I'd like to get my hands on whoever planted that bomb. It might have killed the lot of us."

"So I believe," said Zayev. "It was Alpha, you think?"

Scott looked up sharply. "You know about Alpha, then?"

Zayev smiled wryly. "We have all heard about Alpha, even if it is still a mystery," he said. "It is bad, because it makes for distrust. We never know who is a friend and who is a hidden enemy. Even here, in our Lenin Station, we have our doubts. You could be an Alpha agent, my friend!"

"Some hopes," grunted Alec. "Well, we've just got to keep our eyes skinned."

Ashley Fenton's conference with the Russians took some time, and it was two days before the ferry blasted off again, bound for the Station which by now Scott had started to regard as 'home'. Alec made a routine radio call to Thor, who was taking a spell of duty in the main control room; Scott took the opportunity to practise his piloting—flying a spacecraft was very different from handling an aircraft, as he had found! —and Fenton was busy with his notes when, suddenly, the emergency lights in the panel flashed on.

"What is it?" rapped Fenton.

41

Alec was already at the controls. "Oxygen leak somewhere," he said briefly. "Better get our suits on. It's not serious we'll be docking in twenty minutes."

Scott wasted no time in getting into his suit and connecting up his oxygen leads. Somehow he felt uneasy. Obviously the ferry had been checked and re-fuelled by the Russians; Voronov, Kotov, Zayev and several others had been on board, and he remembered Zayev's comment about a hidden enemy. Yet in itself, a small oxygen leak was of no real account during a short journey, and he felt annoyed with himself for being so suspicious. "All right?" he said. "Pressure's getting a bit low."

"I'll warn Base," said Alec, and called up. "I think Reggie will want to have a look at this. I can't make out what's happened; there doesn't seem to be a leak, but the oxygen's getting out somewhere or other."

Station One was in full view now, and Three had almost vanished in the distance, though from the rear observation window Scott could still see it as a faint speck of light among the stars. "Funny business," he said slowly. "What do you make of it, Ashley?"

Fenton did not reply, and Scott leaned over. "Ashley! Are you all right?"

Still Fenton said nothing. Scott peered through the transparent shield, and let out a gasp. "Alec! Quick —something's wrong. He's turned blue, and I don't think he can hear me——"

Alec spun round. "Check oxygen," he said harshly. "Couple up a spare tank. Hurry!"

Scott knew all about the emergency procedure, and in a few seconds he had a reserve tank connected up to Fenton's suit, but still Fenton did not stir, and Scott felt desperately anxious. "How long?" he muttered.

42

"We can't do a thing until we're back inside. I don't like the look of him."

Alec was already sending out the emergency calls, and the television screen glowed; Thor came into focus. "What is it? Engine trouble?"

"Oxygen leak getting worse," said Alec rapidly "Something wrong with Ashley's tank. Get Constantine to stand by, for Heaven's sake!"

Scott knew that Constantine Londos was probably the most brilliant medical researcher in the world, but he had a cold, clammy feeling that it was too late, and all he could do was to watch Fenton as the ferry drew in with what seemed like agonizing slowness. At last they docked; by now the pressure in the cabin had fallen to zero, and to take off their suits before going through the airlock would have been suicide. Frantically they hauled Fenton through; Londos was waiting, together with Thomson, Vale and Sir Eustace. "Let me look at him," said Londos quietly. 'Help me, please.''

Scott stood back as the Greek doctor pulled away Fenton's helmet and upper suiting. "He is still breathing, which means that there is a chance. I will give him an injection." Scott looked away as the syringe sank into Fenton's arm. "To the medical bay, please. We must hope."

It was half an hour before Londos came back into the control room; by then Vale had begun his check of the ferry, while Thomson had taken charge of Fenton's suit and oxygen tank. "He will live," said Londos, and Scott gave a gasp of relief. "It was dangerous, my friends. He has breathed in a gas which was of no help to him."

Alec stared. "What do you mean? He had the usual oxygen tank——"

"It did not contain oxygen," said Londos slowly. "It had been interfered with, and I suspect that there was also—what is the word?—sabotage in your spacecraft. It was an attempt at murder, and it was nearly successful."

Vale swung in, followed by Thomson. "Murder, you say? Well, you're right. I'll give you the details later, but that ferry was a death-trap, and it can't have been an accident. How is he?"

"He will recover, but it is necessary for him to go down to Earth for at least six months," said Londos. "I myself will accompany him, and I will make sure that he has the best of care. He has been lucky, I think."

"We all were," muttered Scott, and looked across at Thomson. "Alpha?"

"Who else?" Thomson shrugged. "It could have happened here; it could have been worked from Three —we simply can't tell. They were after Ashley all right, just as they were after Reggie. Well, this is something we've got to face. From now on, everyone must be doubly on their guard. We're fighting a war against an enemy we don't know, and it's a war that we've got to win!"

CHAPTER 5

MISSION UNKNOWN

That nightmare journey in the ferry altered Scott's whole outlook. He no longer felt that he was part of a team which was united. As Zayev had said, there was bound to be an atmosphere of distrust, and it was only when he was alone with Nigel, Vale or Thomson that he was able to relax. The one bright spot was that Ashley Fenton came round more quickly than anyone had dared to hope, and in a few hours Londos pronounced him fit for the flight back to Earth. "I'll be back," said Fenton weakly, as he was helped into the airlock. "I won't be down there long, believe me. Best of luck, young Scott—and thanks, Alec; it was a near thing."

Scott knew that his only possible course was to act as naturally as he could, and certainly he had no time to let his nerves get the better of him. Under Vale's direction, and usually with Nigel's help, he made it his business to become familiar with every part of the research programme, and as time went by he found it harder and harder to believe that there was a would-be murderer either on the Station or on Station Three. Then, too, there was the problem of Station Four. After another week, Juan Santos announced that he wanted to go across to a conference with Professor Nagata, the Japanese scientist who was a permanent member of the crew there, and Thomson raised no objection. Rather to Scott's surprise, he was given the task of acting as pilot of the transfer ferry.

"Why me?" he said, when Thomson broke the news. "Of course I'd like to go," he added hastily, "but surely Juan can fly on his own?" He had long since given up the formal 'Dr. Santos'; on Station One, Christian names were very much the usual mode of address.

Thomson chuckled. "I think Juan would be the first to admit that he's the worst pilot in the Solar System. Besides, you haven't been to Four yet, and it isn't a bad idea for you to get some experience without any-

45

one being there to hold your hand. If you press the wrong button and blast off into deep space, don't expect Juan to help you out!"

Scott was only too ready; by now he was fully confident of being able to fly the small transfer-ferries, which were built only for operating in space, and which could never land on the Earth or even the Moon. Inwardly he wished that Nigel could go with him, but obviously Thomson had good reason for sending him on his own, and he had no thought of arguing. Besides, he liked Juan Santos, the cheerful, bald-headed Spanish astronomer whose command of the English language was, at best, imperfect.

"You fly me well?" said Santos, as the two settled into the ferry and Scott made a final check of the controls. "I am not a—a bird-man, you see. I am the valuable cargo."

"I'll let you know if we're on our way to Saturn," said Scott, grinning. "All set? It won't take more than half an hour; they're all ready for us. Who exactly is over there, by the way?"

Santos paused, and waited until Scott had given a burst of power from the motors, sending them gliding away from Station One. "There is, of course, Kaz Nagata—an old friend, you see. Then there is Hamilton Fisher, whom you will know, and there are two more. Dupont is French, you understand. And there is Carl Brand, who is so much in love with his Station that I do not think he ever leaves it!"

"Brand," repeated Scott thoughtfully. "I've never set eyes on him. What does he do?"

"I must make honesty with you. I am not sure," said Santos, and something in his tone made Scott look over sharply. "Brand—well, he is a mystery man; a doctor, I believe. He is not in my department."

46

Scott made a mental note to take a long, hard look at Dr. Carl Brand. Nagata and Fisher he had met during their visits to Station One, and Fernand Dupont had come across twice, thought he was not a talkative kind of person and had little to say to the younger members of the crew. For the moment Scott concentrated on his flying; by now Station Four was looming up ahead, and he could see the docking port, which was much the same as that on his 'home' Station except that it was rather smaller. "I'll call up," he said, and switched on the television link. The screen glowed, and Scott spoke slowly and clearly. "Ferry to Station Four. May I dock? Over."

A face appeared on the screen; Scott guessed that it must be Carl Brand, and he was not impressed. Brand had a short, curved beard, and his face was swarthy and lined. When he spoke, he had a distinct foreign accent which was difficult to place. "All is in order. You may dock."

Scott manoeuvred the ferry gently up to the Station, which was built on the familiar pattern, with a cylindrical hull and several arms jutting out from it. "Docking," he said, and made contact; there was a soft jar, and the ferry came to rest. Santos nodded approvingly. "That was good. You are the splendid birdman, my young friend. Let us enter."

Collecting his various belongings he went into the airlock, and closed the door behind him; the lock would hold only one man at a time, and Scott made a final inspection of the ferry's control system. He remembered Thomson's warning, and even after his few weeks in space he believed in leaving nothing to chance. Then he heard Santos voice. "I am going in, but please to wait. There may be difficulties."

Scott felt mildly surprised, but he waited obediently. Then he heard Brand's gutteral tones. "I am sorry, but at the moment we have no accommodation for more than one visitor. Please return to Station One. I will notify you when Dr. Santos is ready to return."

"But——" Scott felt puzzled. "Look, sir, can't I come over? I'd like to meet you."

"I am sorry. Later it will be possible, but not at the moment. I have been in touch with your commander," said Brand shortly. "You may undock."

Scott thought quickly. He knew that both Thomson and Sir Eustace were anxious for him to see the inside of Station Four—or could it be that they were merely testing Brand's reactions, if indeed Brand were in charge? At any rate, he could hardly force his way in uninvited, and he answered calmly and pleasantly. "I understand, sir. Any message, Dr. Santos?"

"But no. I will call up soon," said Juan Santos. "I think I will ask you to bring me home in a little while. I give you my thanks for the nice ride."

Irritated and bewildered, Scott undocked the ferry and set course back to Station One. He had too much sense to send more than a routine message—after all, Brand and his companions on Station Four could listen-in to anything he said—but as soon as he had re-docked he made his way to the main control room, where he found Thomson and Sir Eustace waiting for him.

"Well, well," said Sir Eustace, as Scott swung himself in. "That was amusing, wasn't it? I don't think you were really a welcome guest, my boy. In fact, one might go so far as to say that friend Brand hated the sight of you."

"I nearly told him to go and jump out of the airlock," grunted Scott. "What should I have done?"

"Exactly what you did," said Thomson. "All the same, I think it's high time we found out a little more. I'll send one of the others across to pick Juan up, and we'll see if they meet with the same reception. Who's it to be, Eustace? Nigel?"

Sir Eustace shook his head. "I think not. Remember, Nigel is my nephew, even though he never trades on it, and if there's anything fishy going on he's bound to be suspect. It had better be either Thor or Alec—Alec, on the whole, because Thor's mainly a communications man rather than a pilot."

It was more than twenty-four hours before the message from Santos came through, but as soon as he called up Alec was dispatched in the ferry; Nigel and Scott were left behind, rather to their annoyance. Vale grinned at them. "Feeling sore?" he said. "I admit that I can't quite make this out. For one thing I can't get through to Kaz Nagata, even though I know him so well. Brand said something about his being ill, though—oh, hang it all, we'll have to wait and see what Juan has to tell us. I think we'll go to the radio room, and listen in."

Thor was on duty in the communications centre, and as Scott came in he heard the tail-end of a conversation; Brand's face was visible on the television screen, and his expression was certainly not friendly. Thor shrugged, and switched off: "Juan is coming back, but Alec was not allowed inside," he said. "I do not understand."

"Neither do I," said Vale. "Better keep tuned in."

"I have the radio circuit," said Thor quietly, "but there is nothing coming through. Alec has told me that he will not transmit again until he docks. There is something strange here."

Minutes passed. Scott went to the observation window, and stared out. Station Four was easily visible—it was moving round Earth in the same orbit as before—and after a few minutes he could make out the ferry; transfer between the two space stations was no more difficult than taking a taxi across London, as Thomson had once remarked. Presently the ferry docked, and Vale went back into the control room; the others followed, leaving Thor behind at the radio. Somehow Scott felt that exciting times lay ahead.

When Juan Santos came in, together with Alec, Scott's feeling of apprehension grew. Santos was not himself. He seemed vague, and unable to collect his thoughts. "Well," said Sir Eustace casually, "how did it go? I hope you gave my salaams to Kaz Nagata."

Santos shook his head. "I—I did not. I did not see him," he said uncertainly. "I am told he is ill. I saw only Brand and Dupont."

Thomson looked up quickly. "Where was Ham Fisher?"

"Fisher? I do not know. Please to excuse me. I must rest," said Santos, still in the same vague tone. "I will sleep, if I may. Thank you."

Thomson began to speak, and then stopped short. "Just as you like, Juan, but I'd like to talk to you when you've rested." He waited until Santos had gone out, and then turned to Alec. "How about you?"

Alec shrugged. "Search me! I spoke to Dupont, but Brand seems to be the man in charge, and I can't make it out. I wonder . . ." He paused. "Look, I may be going crazy, but I wonder if there's something medically wrong?"

"Medically wrong?" repeated Thomson. "What do you mean?"

"Well, Fernand Dupont's a bacteriologist—he's always messing around with those weird 'cultures', as he calls them, and it struck me that he might have let loose some of his pet germs. If so, then he wouldn't want to run the risk of carrying infection across here."

"I see," murmured Sir Eustace. "Interesting theory. There might be something in it, I suppose. All the same, I don't propose to let matters rest. According to International law, any scientist has a right to go to any space station, and that includes both you and Scott. I think I'll do some gentle probing."

It was not until the following 'day' that Santos was himself again, and even then he seemed to have gaps in his memory. "It was—odd," he said slowly; Thomson had called a conference in his cabin, attended by what Sir Eustace had nicknamed the 'inner circle' of Vale, Scott and Nigel. "Oh, they were pleasant, you understand, but I was not able to see Kaz Nagata. I did not feel well, my friends."

Thomson frowned. "You had something to eat, I suppose?"

"But of course. That was only right," said Santos, and paused. "You do not suspect—drugs?"

"I don't know, but it looks rather like it." Thomson glanced across at Sir Eustace. "It's up to you. My instinct is to wait, but I gather you don't agree."

"I'll chew on it," said Sir Eustace blandly. "For the moment we'll sit tight and say nothing, but that doesn't stop us from thinking. You'd better have a medical check-over, Juan, just in case there is something sinister going on."

It was only when Santos had gone out that Sir Eustace dropped his bantering manner. "There are two possibilities," he said, in the crisp tone which meant that he had come to an important decision. "Alec may be right in saying that there is some disease on board Four, in which case we must find out what it is. Otherwise, we're back with our charming friends of Alpha, and if Kaz Nagata won't play ball he may be kept out of the way. I don't like it."

Nigel stared. "But—well, that can't be right. I could take Brand and Dupont as being up to something dirty, but not Ham Fisher. It doesn't make sense."

"No," agreed Sir Eustace. "All the same, remember that Juan didn't actually see Fisher either, which is most peculiar. I have a feeling that anyone forcing their way in may come up against something rather nasty. Do I have to ask for volunteers?"

Vale broke in; he took off his spectacles, glared at them, and jammed them back on his nose. "Force our way in? Just you try it!"

"I don't think that will be necessary, Scruff—not by force, at least," said Sir Eustace mildly. "If you'll listen to me, I'll tell you what is going on in my aged and dim-witted brain. I haven't been idle during the past few hours. I've been on to Central Control, down in Houston, and they in turn have been on to Station Four. The story is that there's a big publicity drive on—as you know, we've been up against the usual moaners who grumble about space stations costing too much, and that we'd be better off spending the money back on Earth, etc., etc. What I've fixed up is a major television programme, with broadcasts from all four Stations, just to show the great bone-headed public that we aren't wasting our time and the tax-payers' cash. Brand and his merry men can't turn that one down, which gives us a perfect excuse to go across."

Scott laughed out loud. "He won't swallow that!"

"Probably not, but it doesn't matter," said Sir Eustace calmly. "You know the influence of television as well as I do, and this is a directive from Houston—it affects Brand as much as the rest of us. Gregory Voronov is happy enough, and I don't imagine that Clyde Warren on Three will have any objection, because there's no American yet born who doesn't enjoy putting his head on the silver screen. Well, my lads, that's the deep-laid plot. Sometime in the near future you two, plus Alec and Thor, are going to turn yourselves into broadcasters, and if Brand tries to keep you out he'll have a great deal of explaining to do."

"If——" began Nigel.

"No 'ifs' about it; I couldn't think of anything better. The snag is that Brand is certain to be on his guard," said Sir Eustace. "I needn't tell you that if he really is mixed up in Alpha he'll stop at nothing, so you'll have to watch your step in no uncertain manner. Enjoy yourselves!"

CHAPTER 6

ON STATION FOUR

Sir Eustace was nothing if not thorough. Also, he knew exactly what he was doing, and Scott could not help feeling amused; only Sir Eustace could dream of forcing an entry into Station Four on the pretext of a television broadcast. "Suppose Brand and Co., simply slam the door in our faces?" he said to Vale, a day or two later when preparations were well under way. "We can't make him let us in."

Vale grinned. "It's not so simple as that. You've heard of 'Komoe', I suppose? K-O-M-O-E: Keep Our Men On Earth. It's a crackpot organization aimed at stopping the whole of space research, and it's been collecting a good deal of support in the last year or two. That's what gave Eustace the idea of a really major broadcast."

"All very well," said Scott, "but . . . well, who's behind Komoe, or whatever it's called? The same people as Alpha?"

"I very much doubt it. Alpha is something really nasty, and I suspect that it's aiming at world control, rather as Hitler did more than half a century ago; unfortunately we don't know who's running it. The Komoe people are different. Most of them are sincere cranks—they believe that if Man began on Earth, he ought to stay there. They don't like spending money on space stations or bases on the Moon." Vale shrugged. "After all, every new science and every new invention has to face people like that; it's human nature. All the same, it doesn't help."

During the next few days Scott made it his business to find out more about Komoe. At least there was nothing secret about it; its members included politicians in almost all countries, to say nothing of the presidents of a couple of African nations. "Stop Wasting Our Money", was the headline in one of the official publications. "Why pour our resources into space when there is so much to be done at home?" The writer went on to develop the theme that men had never been intended to leave Earth, and that even travel to the Moon was against all the laws of nature.

When Vale read the article, he snorted. "Stupid idiot. Why doesn't he take the trouble to do some homework? I only hope he'll have enough sense left to watch our TV spectacular, that's all."

Sir Eustace had left nothing to chance, and, as he modestly admitted, he had bullied every television network in the world into transmitting his programme. The first step was a conference, held in the main control room with almost everyone in the Station present. "We've got things moving well and truly," said Sir Eustace when the team had assembled. "Listen carefully, please. I've arranged for us to talk direct to the other three Stations, so let me know if you have any questions. Switch on, please, Thor."

Thor operated the television controls; there were special circuits to the other three Stations, and Scott recognized the faces which appeared on the screens. From the Russian station, Gregory Voronov raised his hand cheerfully; Clyde Warren could be seen on the American base, and on the third television set appeared the moustached, swarthy face of the French scientist, Fernand Dupont. Sir Eustace beamed at them. "Greetings, gentlemen. Pray silence for our Commander—remember, I'm only one of his juniors. It's all yours, Richard."

Thomson cleared his throat. "I think we all know what we're trying to do," he said. "We've been running into more trouble about finance, and the Komoe people have been making a great deal of noise. We need a vast sum of money to carry out all the work we've planned, and the International Space Agency on its own simply hasn't the funds. What we need is some really good publicity, because people in general tend to get rather bored with space research unless it's regularly crammed down their throats. I imagine we're all agreed on that."

"You're telling me," said Clyde Warren in his strong Southern drawl. "Congress has really been putting on the screws—you'd think they were trying to starve us out. Boy, are they thick in the head!"

Gregory Voronov broke in. "You are not alone, my friend. In the Soviet Union we have a better understanding of science, but even we are in need of money for our projects. Please tell me of the way in which you mean to make this—this great broadcast to the world."

"Certainly," said Sir Eustace. "I take it I'm allowed to air my views, Richard?" Thomson nodded; Scott noted the amused glint in his eyes. "Well, then our message must be—Space Is Essential. We want to explain how we're improving weather forecasting, keeping watch on dangerous tropical storms, exploring the ground for traces of valuable minerals, charting icebergs, handling radio and television communications between every inhabited continent, developing new scientific instruments, studying radiations from space, improving medical techniques—you know; everything we can think of, which is plenty. At the moment I'm not worried about the bases on the Moon, because they can look after themselves for the time being. It's the space stations which matter."

Voronov nodded. "That is sensible, my friend."

"I thought so too," admitted Sir Eustace. "Next, who's to do the actual talking? I gather you've lined up your best commentators by now."

"We have Oleg Kraisky," said Voronov.

"You couldn't do better. Incidentally, I pride myself that I'm not too bad a broadcaster, so I propose to handle affairs from our own Station. Are you happy, Clyde?"

"You bet," said Warren. "I've been on to all our networks, and they're sending up the best broadcasting team they have. They'll be starting any time now, and I'll give them a real good briefing."

"Splendid. That leaves us with Station Four," said Sir Eustace, in what almost seemed an elaborately casual tone. "That's of special importance, because people in general are more bothered about their aches and pains than anything else—and the medical research you've been carrying out, my dear Dupont, is of vital importance. Is there anything really new you can 'put over', to use the popular terms?"

Fernand Dupont shrugged slightly. "I think not. Remember, all our work here is of a very technical nature, and I do not believe that we can play a part in this broadcast."

"I hate to disagree with you, but we really do need something," said Sir Eustace; Scott wanted to grin, but managed to keep a straight face. "Luckily, I think we have the answer. We're very anxious to make an appeal to the younger generation, so what I suggest is that our four lads come across and give a general commentary. We can tune them in to one of the official interviewers, and I think they'll give a good account of themselves. How does that strike you?"

Dupont hesitated. "I—we have no objection. I only say that they must in no way interfere with the experiments that Brand and I are carrying out."

"Of course they won't," said Thomson crisply. "Very well, then; I'll send them across, and you can explain things to them. Well, if we're happy about the main theme, we can get down to discussing details."

There was much to be settled, and the conference went on for several hours, with various other scientists joining in. From the Russian Station there was Boris Kranvich, whom Scott already knew as a brilliant chemist, while from the American base there were comments and suggestions from another familiar visitor, Miles Kenright, whom Scott was to know very well later on. Dupont said little, and of Carl Brand and Hamilton Fisher there was no sign. Nagata, the Japanese commander of Station Four, was not even mentioned, and Scott wondered what had happened to him. Was he ill, or were Brand and Dupont deliberately keeping him out of the way?

"So far, so good," said Sir Eustace, when the television screens had gone blank and the official conference was definitely over. "Now for you lads. I take it that you're ready to go in for this little experiment of ours?"

Thor looked at him meaningly. "There is something behind it, of course," he said in a quiet voice. "If we are to make ourselves useful, we must know exactly what is going on."

"What makes you say that?" asked Thomson.

Thor smiled. "I am no detective, but—well, it makes no sense to send us over to Station Four rather than a well-known television personality. We are not experienced, and neither are we medical experts—but Four is really a medical base. You are not happy about things there?"

"The boy has brains, which is more than I can claim for myself," murmured Sir Eustace. "You're quite right, my dear Thor. Indeed, you are entitled to a cigar or a coconut, whichever you may choose. The fact is that nobody seems to know much about the situation on Four. Kaz Nagata has vanished into the blue as effectively as if he'd been scooped up by a flying saucer, and altogether the Station has been keeping itself to itself. I don't approve."

"Alpha?" said Alec thoughtfully.

"That's what we want to find out. I'm not asking you to do any cloak-and-dagger spy work; simply keep your eyes open, and let me know if you come across anything that's—well, unusual. Above all, try to get hold of Nagata. Call me up as soon as you get there, and keep in touch. You're the expert there, Thor, so you'd better handle that side of it. Any questions?"

Thor and Alec shook their heads; Scott said nothing, but later on he and Nigel were called in for an extra 'briefing', as Sir Eustace put it. Both Thomson and Vale looked serious, and for once Sir Eustace dropped his bantering manner. "Young Thor is no fool, which is just as well—and neither is Alec, come to that. I'm wondering whether we've been fair to them. They may be running into as much danger as you two."

"What kind of danger?" said Nigel. "I don't imagine Brand and Co. will risk trying to kidnap us, or anything like that!"

"No, but there may be other problems. Remember that old cartoon of a Martian arriving on Earth, and speaking to a petrol-pump? 'We haf methods of making you talk, Earthman'. That's why I didn't say anything definite about Reggie's electric screen. The fewer the people who know the details about that one, the better—even though Alpha seem to have got wind of something."

"In that case," said Scott bluntly, "why send Thor and Alec at all? I reckon the two of us can look after ourselves."

"Possibly. But for one thing I want two ferry-

59

rockets over there. Also, there's a certain amount of safety in numbers. The main point is that you'll be in contact practically all the time, so we'll be able to keep tabs on you. There's still time to cry off if you like," he added. "I wouldn't dream of press-ganging you."

Scott and Nigel looked at each other, and burst out laughing. "Some hopes," said Nigel. "I always wanted to try my hand at being a cloak-and-dagger man. This is the big chance!"

The next couple of days seemed to drag by. Work in Station One went on as usual; Juan Santos, now apparently himself again, was busy making arrangements for the replacement of his precious telescope, while Vale spent most of the time in his private laboratory, and Sir Eustace had frequent long-range consultations not only with the other Stations but also with the television networks on Earth. "Everything under control, so far as I can see," he said on one occasion as Scott and Nigel came into the radio room. "I've even had a word with Carl Brand, and he seemed remarkably amiable. He even looked as if he might give me a pleasant smile, though in the end he didn't. I think it's about time you went across for a discussion."

By now Station Four was closer than it had been over the past months; it was moving round Earth at a distance of less than ten miles from Station One, and it showed up as a small cigar of light rather than as a starlike point. It looked very innocent, and as the four boys went through the airlocks into the two ferries, Scott wondered for a moment whether the whole idea of a plot being hatched there was pure imagination. Thor was with him, leaving Nigel and Alec to come in the second ferry. "All set?" said Scott at last. "On our way, pal!"

Thor nodded. Scott made a routine call to Base, and then brought the motors into action; the ferry glided away, and Scott settled down at the controls. "I reckon we're getting nervy. For all we know, old Brand may be as straight as the rest of us."

"I wonder," said Thor quietly. "I wish I knew—but after all, you are in our Commander's confidence, and I am not."

Scott looked across sharply. "What do you mean?"

Thor smiled. "Do you think I am stupid? I am here as an ordinary cadet; if I do well, I will be one of the seniors by the time I'm thirty, but you are something more. Don't worry," he added, and gave a chuckle. "I don't feel at all offended. Remember, I am an Icelander; I come from a small nation which has kept to itself, and I do not—what is the term?—poke my nose into things which I am not supposed to know."

For a moment Scott felt awkward, and he thought it best to say nothing. There was a long silence, broken at last by a call from Nigel in the second ferry. "We'll wait till you're inside, and then dock next to you. Understood?"

"Understood. All well—so far."

It was only a few minutes before they saw Station Four close ahead. Again Scott looked at the docking port, and again he called up; this time Brand answered, and his tone was surprisingly friendly. "Four to ferry. You may dock. Everything is in order."

Scott brought the ferry in, handling it with the ease of an expert, and relaxed as soon as the docking mechanism had clicked into place. Thor went through the airlock; Scott followed, and within a matter of minutes he was inside Station Four. Though he had never been there, the general pattern was familiar enough, and he stripped off his helmet. "Glad to see you," he said to the two men waiting for him. "I'm Scott Saunders. We've talked before."

Carl Brand held out a hand, and gave a smile which did not conceal the hardness of his expression. "I fear we were somewhat inhospitable on the occasion of your last visit," he said in his clipped English. "I will explain fully, I promise you. Dr. Dupont and I are very pleased to make you welcome now."

It all seemed so completely normal that Scott had to remind himself not to be taken off guard. Brand led the way into the main living-room of the Station, and it was not long before Nigel and Alec had docked and joined them. Brand switched on the television screen, and sent out a call. "Station Four to Station One. Do you read me? Over."

The screen glowed, and Thomson's face appeared. Receiving you. Everything in order?"

Brand nodded. "Perfectly, Commander. We may not be really prepared for visitors, but we will do our best to be good hosts." Again Scott wondered inwardly whether his suspicious could be due to anything more than sheer imagination. "We will explain our projects as far as possible, and will call you back. Please keep in touch."

"Understood. Thank you," said Thomson, and nodded casually. "All television networks on Earth have now agreed to transmit, so I'll be able to let you have details of the timings within a few hours."

Brand switched off, and settled himself comfortably; chairs were unnecessary under conditions of weightlessness, and Scott had long since become used to relaxing in mid-air. "I think it best to be quite honest with you," said Brand slowly. "We owe them an explanation, Dupont, and I think we can trust our friends to be discreet. You will, I hope, undertake not to repeat anything I tell you?"

Nigel looked puzzled. "I—well, I don't understand, sir. If we're going to make a broadcast about the work here——"

"Listen," said Brand, and paused. "As you know, Dr. Dupont is a specialist in medical research, and for that matter so am I. We have been conducting experiments upon the effects of long-term weightlessness, and some of these have led us on to some rather surprising results. You can, I hope, understand why we are not anxious to make them public."

"Why not?"

"Because two members of our team have been taken ill," said Bland bluntly. "You may ask why I was unable to allow your colleague to see Professor Nagata. Some weeks ago he complained of feeling unwell, and we very much fear that his health has been affected by some of the drugs which we have been testing. The same has applied to Dr. Fisher. It is extremely unfortunate."

Nigel and Scott exchanged a quick glance, but it was Thor who broke in. "I don't understand," he said. "People have stayed up in space-stations for years on end without being harmed. Commander Thomson hasn't been down on Earth since he first came up, and that must have been way back in the nineteen-eighties——'

"It affects different people in different ways, you must know," said Dupont, drumming his knee with one hand. "Some people can—as you say—'take it', but others cannot. You have no doubt heard of the

63

men who have come up to our Stations and have had to leave again very quickly?"

"I—well, I've heard rumours," said Nigel, "but I didn't take much notice of them."

"That was by intent, not accident," said Dupont. "It is best that you know the full facts, my friend. When the space stations were first launched, it was thought that weightlessness would be quite harmless. Remember that first of all Stations, the American Skylab. The last crew stayed on board for three months, and were in excellent health when they returned. We were very sure then that there was no danger, but since that time there have been men who not only became unwell, but who actually died. There was Vasiliev, of the Soviet Union, to give you only one case."

Nigel frowned. "Vasiliev? I believe my uncle knew him. He was killed in an aircraft crash back home, surely."

Dupont shook his head. "Not so. He died on board Station Two, and there can be no doubt that he was unable to endure conditions of zero gravity. I was myself a colleague of his, and I was with him when he died. We carried out a careful examination of his body, and we found that his blood-group was of a certain special type. At the time we did not realize the significance of this, you understand, but the same thing happened to another astronaut—an American this time: Lee Martin. His blood-group was the same."

"I begin to see," muttered Nigel. "Nagata, then——"

Brand nodded. "Exactly. Professor Nagata belonged to an identical blood-group, and so he was brave enough to volunteer as—as a guinea-pig, if you like. For some months he seemed well, but then he collapsed. You may be sure that we have taken good care of him, but we cannot yet allow him to see anyone or to leave his cabin."

"He's here, then?"

"He is indeed. You may ask why we have not returned him to Earth. The answer is that before his attack, he made us give our word that we would not do so before we had found out the cause of the illness." Brand shrugged. "It was a hard decision, but we had to honour our promise. I have every hope that we will be able to cure him, but I cannot yet be sure. If the truth became known, there would be an outcry at home, and things for us would be made even more difficult."

"I see," said Nigel steadily. "What about Hamilton Fisher, then? Does he belong to the same blood-group, too?"

"His blood is not the same, but it is similar." Brand hesitated. "I must tell you that—that he is dead."

Scott let out a gasp. "Dead! When?"

"Last week. Oh, we tried everything possible to save him," said Brand bitterly. "It was not pleasant, my friend. Not only did we have to see our colleague die, but we were forced to examine his body . . . I will not tell you the details. Now do you see why I could not allow you in our Station when you came to us some days ago?"

Scott knew that his face had gone white. "You let Juan Santos in, though."

"That is true, but he stayed for only a short time, and he was not told the facts." Brand's expression was still calm. "Had I refused, then there would have been suspicions that there is trouble here—and if we are forced to give up our experiments before we have

65

found the answer to our problems, then space research may be set back for a hundred years or more. I will be frank with you," said Brand. "I know Sir Eustace Wainwright well enough to know that he would not have sent you here unless he placed complete trust in you. I am doing the same. You must make your broadcast, my friends, and you must convince the people on Earth that our work is of value to all mankind. What you must not do, on any account, is to tell the truth."

CHAPTER 7

TREACHERY!

Scott thought furiously. Was Brand himself telling the truth, or was he playing a gigantic game of bluff? The man looked sincere and yet there was something about him that Scott did not like. As for Hamilton Fisher—well, Scott had met him several times; it was at least possible that his death had been no accident, and there was only Brand's word that Professor Nagata was still alive. Yet if there was genuine trouble in Station Four, he could see the wisdom of keeping it quiet until the cause of it had been tracked down.

"Pretty awful," muttered Nigel. "Poor old Ham— he was a great guy. Did you—did you bury him in space, sir?"

Brand hesitated, and looked across at Dupont. "Not yet. I told you it was unpleasant—we have to finish all our examinations, you see. Please do not ask me for details. It is too painful, and our work is not yet over."

Scott felt sick, and he saw that both Nigel and Thor were chalky white. Alec swung himself upright. "Mind if I go and check the ferry? I haven't done all the routine stuff yet, and I reckon we may have to get back in a hurry—we don't want to get in the way, and we can spin some yarn good enough for the broadcast. Anyone coming with me?"

"I am afraid this has been a shock," said Brand, in the same calm voice. "I would have given much to be able to hide it from you, my young friends. Let us discuss what is best to tell the people of Earth. We must be very careful."

"We ought to get through to Commander Thomson——" began Nigel.

Brand shook his head. "Not even that. For the moment, it is wise to keep this entirely to ourselves. I am trusting you, and you must put your trust in us. I do not think that this illness, whatever it may be, can be passed from one man to another, but there is always a slight danger, and we must be on our guard. You can check your ferry-rocket later. For the moment, we have work to do."

For the next hour Brand and Dupont went into detailed explanations of the routine work of Station Four; most of it was medical, but some astronomical observation was carried out as well, and Brand was very willing to show all four boys over the observatory, which was remarkably similar to Juan Santos' wrecked installation in Station One. It was a strange time. Scott was still undecided; he was half inclined to take Brand and Dupont at face value, but he had no chance to talk to Nigel, and both Thor and Alec were silent

67

and attentive. Finally Brand produced some food, and apologized for its unattractiveness for all the world like a kindly host. "We do not have good kitchens here," he said, with a smile which seemed genuine enough. "I fear we must—what is the term?—make do with what we have."

Alec had at last gone out to check the ferry; Dupont had stayed behind in the observatory, but even so the control cabin was hardly roomy. Eating under conditions of weightlessness was easy enough, and Scott had long since become used to squirting liquids into his mouth out of gravity bottles; he had not eaten or drunk for many hours—and yet something held him back. He recalled Sir Eustace's words: "We haf methods of making you talk, Earthman." The thought struck him that the food might be drugged. He saw Nigel raise the bottle and drink deeply; Thor did the same, but Scott waited. "Won't be a moment," he said. "Toilet's through there, isn't it?"

Brand nodded, and Scott swung himself through the door into the toilet compartment. The arrangements were conventional enough, and it took him only a second or two to squirt the liquid into the basin and re-fill the bottle with water. When he came back into the control room he felt safe in taking a long drink—water, at least, would be harmless. He felt almost ashamed of himself for being so suspicious, but there was no sense in running any risks.

In was a few minutes later that he saw that Nigel was breathing unusually heavily. His heart pounded—there had been something, then! Thor, too, began to pant, and Scott followed suit, hoping that his acting would be good enough to carry him through. He was certain now that Brand and Dupont were far from being the innocent scientists that they made out, but he also knew that it would be foolish to try to over-power them at the moment. If Thor and Nigel were out of action, he would at least have to wait until Alec came in from the ferry, and there was the un-pleasant thought that Alec might have been tricked in the same way.

Suddenly Nigel gave a loud gasp, and went limp. Thor's eyes were closed, and Scott took a grip on himself; he looked round, shook his head muzzily, and then he too relaxed. Brand straightened up, and eyed the three boys thoughtfully. There was a long pause, and then Scott heard someone come in; he guessed that it was Dupont—in which case Alec must either have been drugged or else taken prisoner. "They are ready," said Dupont, in English; Scott guessed that he and Brand did not speak each other's language. "Let us see what our young men have to tell us. Which one, do you think?"

"Lorrimer," said Brand without hesitation. "He is Wainwright's nephew, and he is the most likely to know. I will give him the injection now."

Scott's brain raced. Would it be best to try a sudden attack, or to wait? He was sensible enough to realize that he would have little chance against two powerful men, but it went very much against the grain to lie still while Brand did his worst. He almost decided to take the risk, but he was too late. "That should be sufficient," said Brand. "Now we must give him a little while before he will be ready to speak."

Another long silence; to Scott it was almost un-bearable. Then Brand spoke again, this time slowly and deliberately. "Lorrimer. Do you understand me?"

"I—I understand." Nigel's voice was thick and slurred. "I understand."

"Good. It is effective," said Brand aside, and then:

"Listen, Lorrimer. You have been told about the protective screen being developed by Dr. Vale?"

No reply, and Brand repeated the question. Still Nigel did not respond, and Brand gave an exclamation of impatience. "We need more drug," he said. "This boy has been well trained."

Again Scott wondered whether he should try a surprise attack, but what was the point? He heard the clink of instruments and a sound that could have been a syringe being filled. There was yet another long pause. "Lorrimer. You understand me?"

"I understand," repeated Nigel, this time in a dull, mechanical tone.

"You have been told about Vale's protective screen," said Brand. "You know its principle?"

"I—I do not know," murmured Nigel. "I do not know."

"As I expected. I knew it was a mistake to try to kill Vale yet," said Brand softly, and then: "Tell me this. Is the screen ready?"

A pause, and Nigel spoke haltingly: "It is not ready. It is not ready."

"When, then?"

"Soon," said Nigel tonelessly. "It will be tested in a few months."

Scott felt desperate. Through no fault of his own Nigel was giving away vital secrets to the man who, as was now only too clear, was a member of Alpha—and there was nothing he could do. The best course was to 'lie low', hope that Brand and Dupont would believe him to be unconscious, and get back to Station One as soon as he could. Brand was speaking again, and Nigel replied. "The screen transmitters are in the second arm. They are hidden from view. I have seen them."

70

"Who else knows about Vale's work?"

"I do not know. I think that only he knows the principle. He is very clever."

"That is certainly true," said Dupont harshly. "No doubt about it, Brand—we must catch Vale himself rather than kill him. He'll need a dangerously large injection before he can be made to talk, but there is no other way of finding out. What shall we do with these brats? Let them go, or dispose of them?"

Scott sensed that Brand had straightened up. "We've drawn all the information we can, but it may be unsafe to let them return to their base," he said slowly. "An accident on their ferry, perhaps—an explosive in the engine compartment, as you suggested. It depends upon how much they remember when they wake up."

Scott risked opening one eye momentarily. Brand and Dupont had their backs to him; Nigel lay motionless, but suddenly Scott realized that Thor, too, had one eye half-open. Thor! Then he also had realized that the food was unsafe—or could there be some other explanation? He opened his eyes again, and saw Thor looking at him.

Scott made a slight gesture, and Thor answered. Brand and Dupont were still bending over Nigel, and Scott made up his mind. "Now!" he roared, and uncoiled himself, hurling himself across the cabin and landing on Brand's back. "Get them—quick!"

Thor was beside him, and for the next few moments there was a wild struggle. Fighting under zero gravity was something new to Scott, and presumably to the others also; but both Brand and Dupont were powerful men, and Scott gasped as he tried to wriggle out of a bearlike grip. "Alec!" he shouted at the top of his voice. "Quick——" He kicked out, and Brand lurched

71

away from him; Thor and Dupont were engaged in a life-or-death wrestling match, but the young Icelander was slimmer and less muscular than his opponent, and Scott began to feel desperate. He dodged as Brand came toward him, and kicked out again, but his feet missed contact, and next moment he was back in that terrifyingly strong grip. Brand's hands were round his throat, and he choked. "I can't—get him off——"

Thor thrust Dupont away, and wrenched at Brand's shoulders. It was touch and go; a red mist swirled in front of Scott's eyes, but suddenly the grip relaxed, and his brain cleared. Then, suddenly, a figure swung in. "Alec!" roared Scott. "On to them, man!"

Alec raised his arm; he was holding a heavy metal bar, and he swung. To Scott's horror he saw the club strike Thor full on the back, and the Icelandic boy gave a cry; next moment Alec was beside Scott, and a fist thudded into his face. This time there was no recovery, and everything went black.

When Scott came round, he was tied hand and foot. Thor was beside him, also bound securely; Brand, Dupont and Alec were looking down at them, their expressions set and grim. Scott blinked. "I—what happened? Alec——"

"Your friend came along at the right moment," said Brand menacingly. "You're as full of tricks as a cageload of monkeys, as you say. Well, you have made your throw—and you have lost."

Scott looked up in utter disbelief. "Alec——"

"It was your own fault," said Alec; his voice was quite unlike that of the pleasant, cheerful boy whom Scott had known. "I didn't want to do it, but you left me no choice. I have my loyalties too."

"But——" Scott gasped; everything seemed suddenly unreal. "You don't mean that—that you're one of them?"

"If you mean 'Do I belong to Alpha?' the answer is that I do," said Alec, and Scott slumped in his ropes. "I didn't want you to know, for obvious reasons, but you took me by surprise. If it's any comfort to you, I'm sorry it had to be this way."

Scott was almost beyond speech. "You—you rat," he breathed at last. "If I ever get hold of you . . . I'll . . ."

"Be sensible," said Brand curtly. "I fear you will be in no position to do anything, my young friend. I need hardly tell you that you are in grave danger of your life, so you had better do exactly as you are told. We will leave you for a while. It is best to wait until you have both come to your senses."

Scott felt horribly sick and ill; he could not move, and he watched bitterly as Brand checked his ropes while Dupont did the same for Thor. Then the three went out, and Scott breathed hard. There was not the slightest chance of breaking free, and in any case they were hopelessly outnumbered.

It was a full hour before Thor came round; his face was badly bruised, and blood had clotted on a cut in his forehead. "I did the same as you," he said in a choked voice. "I thought we might be given drugged food. Where is Nigel? Do you know?"

Scott shook his head miserably, and strained against his ropes. "No idea. Do you suppose that—that they've——"

"Don't think like that," said Thor quickly. "They haven't killed us—not yet, at least—so they may have kept Nigel alive too. If it had not been for Alec, we might have beaten them."

"It's unbelievable," muttered Scott. "I just can't

take it. I suppose he planted that bomb back in Station One—and mucked about with Ashley's oxygen?"

Thor shrugged slightly. "I would think so, unless there are any other Alpha agents back there. Watch me, please."

Scott managed to screw his head round, and faced Thor. The Icelandic boy flicked his eyelids, and Scott realized that he was signalling. Sending Morse code by means of eye movements was a slow business, but it could be done, and Scott read the message without difficulty: "They will be listening. If I can talk to Base, trust me. Make sure that if they give us the chance it is I who calls."

Scott flicked his eyelids back. "Why?"

Before Thor could reply the door opened again, and Brand came back. To Scott's immense relief Nigel was with him, and conscious even though he was pale and sweating in his ropes. Dupont and Alec followed, and Scott scowled; he would have given a great deal to put his fist into Alec's face. There was little left now of the boy with whom he had shared everything over the past weeks.

Brand thrust Nigel down between Scott and Thor. "No, you need have no fear, as yet," he said. "The drug has worn off, as you can see, and if you had not been stupid enough to attack us you would by now be on your way back to your own Station. It was very stupid, was it not?"

Scott looked miserably at Nigel. "Sorry, pal. We tried."

Nigel said nothing; the disaster was so complete that the only possible course was to wait and see what Brand planned to do. Alec looked down. "Better give them some water," he said. "Oh, you can take it this time—it isn't doped. Here you are."

He leaned over, and held out the gravity bottle. Instinctively Scott craned forward, and his teeth closed over Alec's fingers. Alec gave a yelp, and struck out; his hand smacked across Scott's face, and the boy's eyes watered. "All right," said Alec viciously. "If that's how you want it, you can go thirsty." He flung the bottle away, and it thudded against the far wall of the cabin. "Have it your own way."

"Do not be childish," said Brand calmly. "You have found out too much, and you will know that it is quite impossible for us to let you return. On the other hand, I am not fond of killing for killing's sake. Are you ready to listen to reason?"

Nigel writhed. "Go on, then. We'll listen—we've got to."

"I am glad that you realize it. You will be given your lives, on condition that you do exactly as you are told," said Brand. "If not, then you will be put out of the airlock one by one, without spacesuits—and that will mean a death which may be quick, but which will certainly be painful. You will give me your solemn promise that there will be no tricks. Well, Lorrimer?"

Nigel stared at him. "No deal."

Brand shrugged. "Saunders?"

Scott bit his lip. "I can't, and you know it. You can't fool me, Brand—you wouldn't dare let us go, whatever you made us do."

Brand sighed. "A pity, Eiriksson, then? It's your last chance." He turned to the Icelander. "Are you going to be as stubborn as your friends, or will you be sensible?"

75

There was a long pause, and then Thor drew a deep breath. "I—I'll agree. If it's that or being put out of the airlock, I'll do anything you ask!"

CHAPTER 8

A CALL TO DEATH

Brand looked down at the helpless figures, and gave a smile that had no humour in it. "Well, well. At least one of you has a little sense left," he said. "You can have your life, Eiriksson—you may even have your freedom, if you are lucky." He turned to Scott and Nigel. "There is still time for you to change your minds, but I warn you that my patience is wearing very thin."

"Go and chase yourself," muttered Nigel thickly. "Don't believe him, Thor. He'll murder us any-way——"

Scott felt numb with fright, but he did his best to keep his nerves steady. Even at that moment he remembered Thor's message, and he wondered desperately whether the Icelandic boy had any plan which might save them—but what could it be? Brand turned away. "I can't waste any more time on you two. All right, Dupont; put them outside."

Dupont bent down, and took hold of Scott. It was a terrifying moment; Scott knew only too well what would happen to him if he were thrust through the airlock unprotected. He wanted to scream, but somehow or other he managed to control himself. Then he heard Thor's voice. "No. If you kill them, you'll have to kill me too. I may be a coward, but I'm not as yellow as that."

Dupont paused, and looked across at Brand. "Well?"

"What does it matter?" Brand shrugged. "They can wait. As I said, I don't care for killing for killing's sake, and at least they can do no harm. All right, Eiriksson; I'll make a bargain with you. If you obey orders, they can live."

Scott gulped; he wanted to be sick, and his heart pounded wildly. "What do you mean to do with us, even if I obey you?" said Thor, surprisingly calmly. "As you told us, we know too much, and you can't expect us to keep quiet."

"Once we've done what we hope to do, it will hardly matter," said Brand dryly. "Listen carefully, and I will explain. Remember what I say, because a single mistake on your part will be one too many. You may as well give him some water, Kerry—only make sure you don't get bitten this time!"

Alec held out a gravity bottle, and Thor gulped down some of the liquid. Then Brand settled himself down, and began to speak in much the way that he might have lectured to an audience of students. "There is no point now in keeping anything from you," he said. "You will know that Alpha is a very efficient organization; it has its agents everywhere, and we happen to be three of them. I won't bore you with explaining just what our ambitions are, because it would take too long, but you may be sure that within a few years from now we will have more strength than any dictator has ever had in the history of the world. We began in a small way, but we have been building up our power very quickly indeed."

Scott broke in. "Who's the head of it?"

"That does not concern you. I would not tell you even if I knew," said Brand. "The main point is that we need all the scientific knowledge we can get, and there are only a few leading scientists who are ready to work with us. Your friend Vale is, unfortunately, not one of them."

"I should think not," breathed Nigel.

"If you irritate me, you will be removed," said Brand coldly. "I advise you to keep silent. Vale is undoubtedly the most brilliant electronics expert now living, and we know that he has been working upon a screen which will make any space station too strong to be attacked. Our people have been trying to produce something along the same lines, but so far with little success. This is why we must have Vale himself."

"But——" began Thor.

"I know what you are going to say: he would never willingly give us the information we must have," said Brand. "Luckily, there are methods of—persuasion. When I told you that we had been carrying out medical experiments, I was being quite truthful. Two of our subjects were, needless to say, our colleagues here on Station Four—Nagata and Fisher."

"So that's it," breathed Nigel. "You doped them, and then scuppered them——"

"We have not scuppered them, as you put it. Nagata has been under drugs for some time, and so for that matter has Fisher; I am afraid I was not being honest with you when I told you he had died. As a matter of fact, both he and Nagata are within a few yards of you at this moment, though I fear you would be unable to get any sense out of them. They were stupid, and they would not listen to reason. They may recover eventually, I suppose."

"You brute," muttered Nigel.

Brand smiled again. "All in the interests of science, my friend, and in any case it is Dr. Dupont who has been conducting the main research; I do not pretend to have sufficient knowledge of such matters. It is only recently that we have been able to perfect a drug which will force complete information out of—well, the victim, if you like. In fact, Lorrimer, you were privileged to be the first unwilling subject of it. I had hoped that you would be able to tell me more than you were able to do, but that is hardly your fault."

Alec broke in. "Why are you telling them all this?"

"Perhaps because I am rather proud of what we have been able to do," said Brand thoughtfully. "At least we have been more than a match for all the world's intelligence agencies, and that includes your friend Wainwright. I doubt if he will be pleased to find that he has had one of our men in his own team. As a matter of interest, Eiriksson, did you have any suspicions?"

Thor shook his head. "No. You took me in, Kerry."

"All our men are well trained," said Brand. "In an organization such as ours, we cannot afford to make mistakes—and any of our agents who fails to measure up to our standards is liable to meet with an unpleasant fate. To continue. It would have been useless to have made any attempt to capture Vale earlier, because I realize that no threats would have made him tell us anything at all. He and I once worked together before the space stations were launched, so I know him well. Indeed, we regarded him as so dangerous that we were ordered to remove him, and I am extremely glad that we failed. Now, at last, we have the means of drawing everything from him. This is where you can help us, Eiriksson."

79

Thor looked blank. "How?"

"By persuading him to come across to Station Four," said Brand crisply. "This is what you must do. You will be seated at the television panel—securely tied up, of course, but I am sure we can make everything appear normal. I will call up Station One, and ask to speak to Vale. Your task is to tell him that there is trouble here, and that you need his help as a matter of urgency. Provided that he has no suspicions, he will come, and that is all we want."

Thor stirred uncomfortably. "I—I can't do it. You're asking me to turn traitor, and we've had enough traitors already. It's too much!"

"The choice is yours," said Dupont harshly. "If you do not agree, or if you make any attempt to warn Vale —well, you will be last through the airlock; you can watch your friends die first."

Brand nodded. "Quite so. I can promise you an excellent view. You will be taken to the observation window, and you will be able to see exactly what happens. Lorrimer first, I think, and then Saunders—it will not be pleasant. Your turn will come very soon afterwards. I will give you exactly three minutes to make up your mind."

Thor twisted his head round, and looked desperately first at Nigel and then at Scott. "What shall I do? I—I can't think! Brand, if you've any decency left in you——"

Nigel said nothing. Scott stared, and then he saw Thor's eyelids flick again. Three long blinks; then long, short, long—the Morse for "O.K." Scott made up his mind. "Get him over," he said in a strangled voice. "I can't face it. Go on!"

He saw the look on Nigel's face, and he flushed; suppose he was wrong? There was a silence that seemed as if it would never end, and then Brand spoke again. "One minute left. You will have no second chance. I am not bluffing, Eiriksson; after all, you will be of no further use to us if you do not co-operate."

Thor gave a sobbing cry. "All right—I'll do it. Call up, then, and get it over!"

"Not so fast," said Brand coolly. "If you talk to him while you're in that state, you will deceive nobody, and your life depends upon how well you act. If Vale comes across unprepared, your life will be same. Drink this, and pull yourself together."

Thor breathed hard, and swallowed the liquid. "I'm ready," he said at last. "Go on."

Still Nigel said nothing, but his eyes were hard and contemptuous. Scott watched as Thor was hauled over to the control table and tied to the chair; his feet were firmly shackled, and a rope was passed around the lower part of his body. "You will have your hands loose," said Brand, "but I warn you not to try any tricks. I think you understand."

Thor nodded. "I—I understand. Suppose he won't come?"

"Then you go through the airlock," said Brand, without a trace of emotion. "I've already told you that we have no patience with failures. On second thoughts, you'd better say that the television circuit is out of action, the sound radio will do just as well. Tune in."

Thor looked quickly round. Scott felt hopeless; if Thor had meant to try the Morse code he had been outwitted, and there seemed no other possible way to send a warning without discovery. Nigel struggled vainly in his ropes; Alec stood by, and it was hard to credit that only an hour or two before he had been classed as a friend.

"Thor Eiriksson to Station One," said Thor in the microphone, and Scott was taken aback at the steadiness of his voice. "Calling Station One. Come in, please. Our television is out of action."

The receiver crackled, and a familiar voice came through. "Thomson to Station Four. I am receiving you loud and clear. Why cannot you use the television circuit?"

"There has been a breakdown. We are carrying out repairs, but it will take a few hours," said Thor, and looked at Brand; Brand nodded. "May I have permission to speak to Dr. Vale, please? It is urgent."

"What's the matter? Explain yourself," came the reply, and Scott's heart leaped; the voice was Vale's. "We've been sitting around waiting for you to call us. I thought we told you to keep in close touch—I've been calling and calling. You ought to have more sense. Where are you?"

"I'm in the radio room," said Thor. "There's nobody else here; I wanted to talk to you without being overheard. Reggie, you'll have to come across. We need you, and we need you now."

"What the blazes do you mean?" rapped Vale. "Don't blather, boy. Speak out."

"Give me a chance, then. Remember what the old Sagas say," said Thor, and added a few words in Icelandic. 'Keep your counsel and be patient!'—that comes from the Saga of Erik the Red. You needn't worry about anyone here; they're doing all they can, but there's some interference with the electronics, and we can't make out where it's coming from. Carl thinks it may be deliberate." Scott noted the use of Brand's Christian name, and he breathed hard; if Thor were acting, he was doing so with superb skill—and yet what was the point?

"Oh," said Vale, in a different tone. "I begin to see. Why can't Brand talk to me himself, then?"

"Because he's outside, tinkering with the television aerial," said Thor. "I can't tell you more now, because if I'm right there may be someone listening in. Come over in the ferry, and we'll put you in the picture."

Thomson broke in. "You're certain of your facts?"

"Yes. The interference seems worse every time we pass over Australia," said Thor; his voice was still steady, and Scott felt utterly bewildered. "Carl thinks it may be jamming. It might be anywhere around there—even from China, I suppose— —"

He broke off. Nigel struggled desperately, and opened his mouth to give a yell, but Dupont was too quick; he clapped a hand over the boy's face, and Nigel could do no more than gasp and splutter desperately. "That was a call from outside," said Thor crisply. "I'll have to go, Reggie. Can you come across?"

"All right," snapped Vale. "If we're dealing with people on Earth rather than in space, there's no reason why I shouldn't team up. Tell Brand I'll be over as soon as I can get the ferry fuelled up. I'll have to take the large one—the others are due for checking. Out."

"Understood. Out," said Thor, and switched off. "Look, I've done as you told me; let him go!"

Dupont straightened up, and took his hand away from Nigel's face. "You were very near to death," he said grimly. "If you had managed to shout, I would have strangled you. Young fool!"

"I may be a fool, but I'm not a traitor," breathed

83

Nigel, and stared at Thor. "You're no better than—than Kerry. Do you realize what you've done, man? Reggie Vale will walk right into the trap, and once he's under that fiendish drug he'll blab. You yellow skunk!"

Thor drew back. "I have saved your life. You should be grateful."

Dupont shrugged. "Well, these brats are of no further concern to us. I suggest that we put them outside here and now. There is no sense in keeping them alive," he said. "You are in command, but I think we should waste no time."

Brand gestured. "And let Vale see them drifting in space—dead? Don't be stupid, Dupont. Besides, they may be useful even now. We will need more subjects for our experiments, and two of these boys at least have been in space for many months. No; I will keep my promise for the time being. Silence them, and see that they are well tied up. They will keep."

"I'll see to that," said Alec, and gave Scott a rough kick that made the boy wince. "I'll teach you to bite! I've half a mind to thrash you here and now."

"Try not to be childish," said Brand impatiently. "Vale will be with us before long, and we must make sure that we are ready for him. Leave the Icelander here; we may need him, and he seems to have more intelligence than the other two. Hurry."

Alec tested Nigel's cords, and tied a gag over his mouth; then he did the same for Scott, pulling the cords painfully tight. Dupont picked Nigel up and went through the door; Alec followed, ramming a cloth over Scott's face and knotting it. Scott gasped. He wondered whether he was to be taken to the airlock, but Alec steered him down the main corridor, and into a small cabin at the end of one arm of the Station.

"In you go," said Alec roughly, and Scott was thrust away with such force that he cannoned against the far wall with a jolt which knocked the breath out of him. The door slammed shut, and Scott spun round helplessly.

It took him some minutes to clear his brain and blink the sweat from his eyes. Then he let out a cry of amazement. The light was dim, but sufficient for him to see across the cabin—and he and Nigel were not alone; two more trussed-up figures were there. Somehow or other he managed to turn himself round, and gave a gasp. One of the prisoners was Professor Nagata, still the official commander of Station Four. The other was a tall, bald-headed man whom he recognized instantly as the missing American scientist, Hamilton Fisher.

CHAPTER 9

"INTO THE AIRLOCK!"

Both Nagata and Fisher looked in poor shape, at least so far as Scott could see in the gloom; the outer window was not fully shuttered, though the electric lights in the cabin had been switched off. Nagata hung limply clear of the wall, but Fisher's eyes were open, and apparently he had managed to loosen the gag to one side of his mouth. "Gee! you too," he said in a hoarse whisper. "We're sure in a spot, young Nigel. They won't pull any punches."

Nigel writhed helplessly; Scott managed to steer himself across the cabin by jerking his cramped legs against the far wall. An idea had come to him—not likely to be of much real help, but better than nothing. If Fisher had his mouth free, there was at least a chance that he might be able to loosen some of the knots that Alec had tied so expertly.

He flicked Morse with his eyelids, and to his relief Fisher understood. "Reckon you're telling me something. Spin round toward the window, and I'll read you. I don't expect there's any hurry," said Fisher bitterly. "I've been cooped up for days, and Kaz for even longer. He's out for the count; those swine have been using him as a test for their devilish dope."

Scott manœuvred himself round. "Try to bite my rope," he flicked. "Get my hand free."

Fisher grunted. "With my false teeth? Talk sense, buddy. I can't chew a rump steak, let alone a rope."

Scott flicked back. "My gag, then."

He tapped the wall gently—luckily he could move his feet a few inches—and managed to float across until his face was almost touching Fisher's. As he came up Fisher craned his head forward, and grabbed at Scott's gag; then he began to chew at it, rather in the manner of a dog worrying a bone. Somehow the whole situation was so comic that in spite of the circumstances Scott could not help bursting into a choked laugh, and Nigel joined in. "You've sure got guts," muttered Fisher. "Keep still, or I won't have a chance."

The minutes passed as Fisher tugged and tugged at the gag. It was slow work, and Scott had almost begun to lose all hope when he felt the knot beginning to slacken. At last it came loose, and Scott blew against it with all his force, sending it floating gently across the cabin. "Phew! that's better—thanks. All right?"

"I reckon I'll need a new set of snappers," said Fisher. "See what you can do, Scott. Better take me first, because my ropes have been on me for what seems an age, and they're probably slacker than Nigel's."

"Right. Twist round if you can," said Scott. "Let's hope none of the brutes come in. If they do, try to kid them that we're all out for the count."

Fisher pushed against the wall, and Scott did his best to see if any of the knots were at all loose. "I'll have a go at your wrist," he said. "Don't wriggle it around until I tell you."

There was nothing false about Scott's teeth, but the rope was so securely tied that for the best part of half an hour he made no progress. There was no time to tell Fisher what had been happening, and for that matter there was no need; unless they could free themselves before being interrupted, they would be powerless. "Try to move it," he said at last. "I believe it's starting to give."

Fisher obeyed, and then, suddenly, the knot came undone. "Good boy," said Fisher quietly. "I guess I can fix it now." It didn't take him long to undo the other knots, and soon he was stretching his cramped limbs thankfully. "Now I know what a turkey feels like when it's trussed up before Christmas dinner," he said ruefully, as he set to work on Scott's ropes.

It was not long before both Scott and Nigel were free. "Boy! What wouldn't I do to that pair if I could get my hands on them," said Fisher. "I'd hammer them well and truly before turning them in."

"That goes for me too," muttered Nigel. "I've a lot stored up for both of 'em, but Alec's the one I really want to bash. What about Professor Nagata?"

Fisher was already sawing away at the ropes round

the Japanese scientist. "I'll get him loose, but he won't be a lot of good yet awhile. He's had so much dope that he's in a real bad way. Look, you'd better tell me what's been going on."

Nigel explained, as quickly and clearly as he could, while Scott went round the cabin hoping against hope that he might be able to find some way of escape. The door was locked—or, at least, it refused to budge when he put his shoulder against it; the observation window was made of tough plastic many inches thick, and in any case all the air in the cabin would rush out if they broke the protective screen. "Not much we can do," said Fisher at last. "We'll have to sit tight and wait until they come to get us. Then we'll rush them, and hope for the best."

"But——" began Nigel. "Reggie Vale's probably getting ready to come over. He won't suspect a thing, thanks to that Icelandic rat, and they may drug him before they even think of coming back here. Anyway, we've no guarantee that they'll come back at all. They may just leave us here for keeps."

"They want us as specimens for their drugs," said Fisher dryly. "Oh, I get the point—but what else can we do? We can't melt cold steel, and there's no way out except for the door. Are you sure your pal let you down?"

"He may not have done," said Scott. "I don't know. He gave me the tip that he had some plan worked out——"

"Don't kid yourself," said Nigel scornfully. "You heard it as clearly as I did. He spun Reggie a yarn that sounded right on the level, and Reggie swallowed it. He couldn't very well do anything else, I suppose."

Scott shrugged; much though he hated to believe that Thor had lost his nerve, there seemed to be no other explanation, and for the moment he said no more. Again he prowled around the dimly-lit cabin, but with the same result, and all three settled down to wait.

Time passed. The strain was almost unbearable, and there was little to say; the thought of Vale walking straight into the trap was frightening, but there was no chance of raising the alarm. Nigel still had his torch, and both he and Scott examined the door again and again, but it seemed to be bolted as well as locked —as Brand had said, Alpha was nothing if not efficient. Fisher had almost recovered, but Nagata was still unconscious, and when they tried to rouse him they had no success. "He'll need a lot of doctoring before he's fit again," commented Nigel. "If he's been pumped full of dope, it'll be a long job."

"Always assuming that we get out of this jam," said Scott thickly. It was becoming more and more of an effort to keep cool. "They—hold on. Listen."

All three tensed. Sounds were coming from outside, and then, slowly, the door began to swing open. Nagata was in full view, and his ropes dangled limply; there was no time to swing him out of the way, and the only hope was to attack as quickly as possible. "I hope it's Alec," was the thought that ran through Scott's mind—and then he sprang, Nigel close behind him. There was a muffled shout, and then Scott's hand was clapped across the man's face; Fisher clenched his fist, and struck. The man collapsed, and Nigel pulled the door until it was almost shut. "Quiet," he breathed. "One down and two to go. Which of 'em is it?"

"Dupont," said Fisher in an equally low tone. "Let me look at him. I reckon he's knocked silly, but we'll take no chances. Better tie him up."

Dupont stirred, and opened his eyes, putting up his hand to tear at the cloth which Scott was cramming into his mouth. Fisher did not hesitate. He drew back, clenched his fist again, and lashed out with every ounce of his strength. The blow landed full on Dupont's jaw, and the man sagged. "That'll fix him for long enough," said Fisher rapidly. "Not nice, but he asked for all he got. Now for the others, before they get wise to us."

Cautiously he opened the door; the corridor of the arm leading down to the main hull of the Station was empty, but the lights were on, and there was no possible hiding-place. "They'll be in the control room," muttered Nigel. "If they aren't on their guard, we've a chance!"

Scott looked round for a weapon, and picked up a metal bar which had been lying against the outer wall, held there by one of the usual magnetic clips. Fisher was already half-way down the corridor, and Nigel and Scott followed. There was no time to be lost, particularly if Vale was already on his way.

Station Four was much smaller than their own base, but the layout was exactly the same apart from the fact that there were only two main arms, one leading to the observatory and docking port and the other to the room they had just left. There was no need to 'walk'; they could ease their way along without their feet touching either the floor or the walls, but it was slow going, and they dared not utter a sound. True, they were three now against only two, but there was every likelihood that both Brand and Alec were armed, and an old-fashioned gun was just as effective on a space station as it was on Earth. At last they reached the main door of the control-room, and they paused. Scott gestured. "Wait or rush 'em?" he mouthed.

Fisher held up his hand. "Wait," he mouthed back. "They're bound to come out sometime, and that'll be our big chance."

The door was solid and soundproof, and there was no way of telling who was inside the control room. Thor, presumably, was still tied up, but there was always the unpleasant possibility that Brand or Alec might be outside, in which case everything might depend upon whether or not they were carrying either guns or else the electric 'stunners' which caused temporary paralysis to anyone hit with them. The wait seemed endless. When the door swung open it took them by surprise; Scott saw a tall figure swinging out, and once more he made a leap, but this time he was not quick enough. "On to him!" roared Fisher, as the man thrust back into the control room. "Give him the works!"

Scott and Nigel burst in, and saw that there were only two people in the room—Thor, still trussed and helpless, and Alec Kerry, crouching back against the far wall and pointing a wicked-looking gun at them. "Stay where you are," said Alec, his voice raised in a snarl. "One move, and I'll finish you off. Brand! Brand, I've got them—I'm in the control room——"

"You can't shoot three of us at once," said Fisher coolly. "Better give up, sonny. You've lost this trick."

"Think so?" Alec edged forward, and pointed toward Thor. "He'll be the first. Don't think I'm bluffing—he'll get a bullet through the head if you lift a finger. Brand!"

Scott looked frantically at Nigel. Alec meant what he said, and at point-black range there was no chance that he would miss; Thor was helpless, and it could be only a matter of seconds before Brand came back. Yet what was the alternative? Scott did the only possible thing, and he acted so quickly that he gave himself no chance to think of the consequences. His foot was braced against the wall, and he thrust out with every atom of his muscle-power, aiming at the gap between Thor and the pointing gun. There was a loud report, and he felt a searing pain in his arm; he cried out, and realized dimly that he had been hit. Again Alec fired, but both Nigel and Fisher were rushing him now. Suddenly there was a brilliant flash of light, and Scott felt something else—a numbness in his body that could be due only to one of the small but deadly electric stunners. The room whirled crazily around him, and everything went black.

Hours later, so it seemed, he came round. His arm ached furiously, and so did his head; he heaved, and did his best to keep back the sickness which threatened to overwhelm him. The control room was a shambles. The radio panel and the television screen were shattered and smoking; evidently they had caught fire, and they were certainly out of action. Thor was stretched out against one wall, and of Nigel and Fisher there was no sign. Scott gulped. "What happened? I can't see!" His eyes were sore, and he realized that his forehead was caked with blood from a deep cut; his right arm was useless, and he felt too ill to move.

"You went just one step too far," said Brand's cold, hard voice. "I don't pretend to know how you got out, but you won't have the chance to do it again. He's all yours, Kerry. If you want to thrash him during the last few minutes of his life, I won't stop you."

Alec raised a hand, and struck Scott across the face. "Pity you tried to be so clever," he said. "You've got guts—I'll give you that—and you're going to need them. You're no more use to us."

Scott blinked; he was still in a daze. "Nigel! What have you done with him?"

"Put him back where he came from, and made sure he was properly fixed this time," said Brand. "Fisher, too. If it's any comfort to you, they won't be killed yet awhile; I have several experiments to carry out first, though I doubt whether they'll enjoy them. Shall I give them your best wishes?"

Scott stared. "I don't understand."

"Then I will explain," said Brand grimly. "Both Lorrimer and Fisher are physically sound, so they will make excellent subjects, but you are not. Your arm would take a long time to heal even if it had the opportunity. We need only two subjects—and you, my friend, are the odd man out. In precisely five minutes, you'll be going through the airlock—and you won't be wearing a spacesuit."

CHAPTER 10

THE TERMS

Scott drew a deep, shuddering breath. Brand was not bluffing; he meant exactly what he said, and even though Scott was untied he was in no shape to put up any kind of a fight. He eased himself round until he was facing Alec. "I can't stop you, but it won't do you much good in the end," he said, hoping that he sounded less frightened than he felt. "Look, it's only a few hours since we were sharing everything——"

For a moment Alec looked uncertain, but then his expression hardened again. "No use, Saunders. I don't particularly want to kill you, but that's the way things are working out, and it's your own fault."

"My fault!" breathed Scott, and did his best to struggle up. "What did you expect me to do? Turn yellow?"

"Your Icelandic friend did," said Brand in his dry voice. "We're wasting time, Kerry. Get him out of the way. We don't want him in full view when the ferry comes across—and incidentally you'd better be the first to go and meet Vale; he won't suspect anything, but I still don't know whether he trusts either me or Dupont. Get busy."

Alec grabbed hold of Scott's limp form, and coiled a rope round him; Scott's right arm was blood-clotted and helpless, and he felt horribly faint. "It'll be quick enough," said Alec. "I'll put you in the lock and leave the pressure up until everything's sealed. Then I'll open the far door, and the air will rush out in a few seconds. Better than reducing the pressure slowly, so that you'd take minutes to choke!"

"Kind of you," said Scott, still in a steady voice. "You—you can't be serious, Alec!" He used the Christian name deliberately, desperately hoping that it would awaken a spark of decency; but Alec said nothing, and pushed Scott down the corridor into the docking port. "Right," he said roughly, and opened the airlock door. "You'll have a couple of minutes yet. Better make the most of them."

The inner door swung shut; the light in the wall was still on, and Scott stared around. Only the outer wall lay between him and the airlessness of space, and once Alec operated the controls which would open the port—well, that would be the end. Scott had heard stories of men whose vacuum-suits had failed, and he did his best to keep a grip on himself. The best he could hope for now was that it would be all over before he had time to realize what was happening. "Rotten way to finish up," was the thought which shot through his mind. "And I'll never know the end of it!"

The silence was complete. Scott kept his eyes fixed on the outer door, waiting for it to move. Still nothing happened; was Alec deliberately keeping him in suspense, or was there some other reason? Scott wanted to scream; he knew that he could not keep his self-control for much longer. And then, suddenly, there was movement—not of the outer door, but of the inner panel which led back to the interior of the Station. Scott let out a cry, and twisted round.

"You're lucky," said Brand curtly. "Vale will be docking in a few minutes, and it wouldn't be wise to tip you out until he's—well, enjoying our hospitality. All right, Dupont; get him out of the way."

Dupont, one side of his face swollen dramatically where Fisher had hit him, stepped forward in silence, and thrust the gag back across Scott's mouth. He pushed him roughly out of the airlock down the corridor leading to the control room. Scott winced; his arm was throbbing more and more furiously, but at least he was alive. He made no attempt to ask questions; it was best to wait quietly, particularly as he was too badly hurt to put up even a token fight.

Dupont kicked him into the control room, and Scott drifted helplessly across to the far wall; Thor, he saw, was still there, and still tied up. Then Dupont went out, and there was a long pause. The gag across Thor's face covered his eyes as well as his mouth, so there was no chance of any more Morse signalling,

95

and Scott did not even know for certain that he was conscious.

Suddenly there came a tell-tale jolt; a ferry had docked. Vale was here, then, and presumably completely off guard. Scott bit at his gag; if he could manage even a choked shout it would be better than nothing, but Dupont had been too thorough, and the most Scott could manage was a moaning sound. He knew, too, that it would be Alec who would be sent to meet Vale in the docking port, and so far as Vale was concerned Alec was still a trusted member of the crew.

Still there was no sound—until, suddenly, pandemonium broke loose. From the direction of the docking arm there came a series of shouts; then there was a shot, a loud cry and then the noise of what seemed to be a chase. Abruptly the door of the control room swung back, and a space-suited figure came in, followed by another. "Two of them, anyway," said a familiar voice, and in a matter of seconds Scott's gag and ropes were free; Thor was released at the same time, and opened his eyes, blinking in the sudden light.

"Most interesting," said Sir Eustace Wainwright, taking off his helmet and beaming cheerfully. "Quite a family party, isn't it? If—Scott, you're hurt. Let me look."

"I'm all right," muttered Scott weakly; the reaction was almost too much for him, and he was close to collapse. "What's happened?"

Vale pushed his helmet back, and straightened up. "Thor's not much knocked around, at least. Better make sure we've rounded up the whole nest of them before we start any first-aid; they're as slippery as snakes, and a great deal more dangerous." He called out. "Gregory—Juan. Have you collared all three?"

"Look out for—for Alec," gasped Scott. "He's been in Alpha all along. If it hadn't been for him, I reckon we could have fixed this lot on our own——"

"My dear fellow, I know all about Alec Kerry," said Sir Eustace mildly. "Oh, I admit that he took me in as completely as he deceived everyone else, and I now realize that I'm even more stupid than I thought, but once we had the tip-off from Thor we were more than ready for him. Be careful of that arm. We'll get you over to the hospital section as soon as we've cleared things up."

"It was pretty quick thinking," broke in Vale. "Wake up, Thor my lad; it's all over bar the shouting. Take it easy."

Scott stared. The Icelandic boy was still dazed, and Scott wondered whether he had been given a shot of Brand's drug. "How did he do it, then? We were with him all the time, and we didn't hear him say anything."

Vale chuckled. "That's where you're wrong, as you might have realized if you'd had the sense to listen out. When Thor came on the air, he quoted something from the Icelandic sagas—only it wasn't quite what the old bards wrote! As I believe I told you once, I can speak Icelandic pretty well, and in those few sentences Thor gave us the whole story. Not bad, eh?"

Scott looked up, and burst into a laugh. "I'll say not. Old Brand and his gang never spotted it. I bet they'll be sick when they find out how they were fooled," he said. "You know they were just going to push me through the lock?"

"We had an idea that they might be planning some-

D

thing of the sort," admitted Sir Eustace. "That's why we were in so much of a hurry. Unfortunately we had to wait until the big ferry was fuelled up, because we wanted to bring quite a party across with us, and both Gregory Voronov and Juan Santos were more than ready to come. If you're really all right, I think we'd better go and supervise the mopping-up operations."

Vale swung across to the main door, and jammed it open. "I know we knocked two of them out with the stunners. Dupont was one, and that rat Kerry was the other. That only leaves Brand himself, and I hardly think he'll get far. Have you got him, Gregory?"

Gregory Voronov made his way down the main corridor. "We haven't got him yet," he said grimly, "but we know where he is, and he's not getting out. I don't believe he'll put up a fight. I knocked his gun out of his hand, and he didn't have a stunner. He's shut himself up in one of the far cabins, and unless he had a spacesuit tucked under his arm that's where he will stay. Where are the others? Nigel, I mean, and Ham Fisher?"

"In——" Scott began, and then stopped short; a frightening thought had come to him, and he swallowed hard. "They're tied up—Nagata too. We made a break for it, but we hadn't a hope——"

Vale let out a roar. "You young idiot! why didn't you tell us straight off? If Brand gets at them before we do, he'll be capable of anything. Which cabin was it?"

"Arm Two," muttered Scott. "Right at the far end."

Vale swung himself out, and Sir Eustace followed, moving with a speed and agility quite unlike his usual leisured calm. Scott tried to follow, but any movement made him sick and dizzy, and he realized that there was little he could do. "I can help you," said Thor

98

quietly. "You thought I had played the coward, did you not?"

Scott shook his head weakly. "Not really. Nigel did, I think; I couldn't tip him off, and anyway I didn't know how you were going to work it. Better go and help the others. I'm no good yet."

"What do you mean? Remember, I have been out out of touch," said Thor, with a dry grin. "I tried to wriggle free, but Dupont hit me on the head. Where is Nigel?"

"Tied up in the far cabin, and that's where Brand has gone," said Scott dismally. "Give me a hand, then."

It was not far to the cabin where he had been kept prisoner, but it took Thor some minutes to ease him down, and to Scott every movement was sheer agony. As he had feared, the cabin door was firmly shut, and Vale, Sir Eustace, Voronov and Santos were clustered outside it. "Difficult," said Sir Eustace softly. "Very difficult. Really, I seem to have made every possible mistake . . . Gregory, I think you'd better go and make sure that those other two beauties are dead to the world. They won't come round for at least an hour, but we may as well give them an injection that will put them out for longer than that. I have a feeling that the tables have been well and truly turned on us, and we've quite enough trouble already."

Voronov nodded briefly, and made his way back down the corridor. "I clouted both Kerry and Dupont with the most powerful electric stunner I could find," explained Sir Eustace calmly. "If I'd managed to hit Brand as well, we might all have been packing up by now. As things are—well, I don't know. The one saving grace is that the brute can't possibly get out."

"Neither can the others," muttered Scott. "Nigel's in there——"

"You needn't tell me that." Sir Eustace looked hard at Vale. "No chance of pumping in gas or anything of that kind, Reggie?"

"How? Even if we had any cylinders here, there's no way of pumping gas in," said Vale shortly, and hammered on the door. "Brand! Brand, can you hear me?"

There was no reply, and Vale hammered again, pounding the heavy door until his knuckles were red. "No use," said Juan Santos. "You cannot break it down, my friend. We must keep calling."

"He can hear me all right," snapped Vale. "He's trying to bluff it out, I suppose. Brand! Speak up, man!"

A pause, and then Brand's voice came through, muffled but quite audible. "What do you want?"

"You," said Vale bluntly. "You may as well come out. We'll simply wait until you do."

"Indeed? But I think you have forgotten something," said Brand, his tone controlled and icy. "It is true that I cannot escape, but I am not alone. I have no less than three companions, and only one of them is unconscious. If you doubt me, I will ask them to speak. You first, Lorrimer."

Another pause, and then a soft thud which could only be a blow of fist upon flesh. There was a choked cry, and Brand spoke again. "Fisher, then?"

"You dirty skunk!" they heard Fisher say hoarsely. "The boy's hurt. Keep your hands off him!"

Scott bit his lip until it bled. He knew, only too well, that Nigel, Fisher and Nagata were in deadly danger, and he had an insane wish to throw himself against the door and try to batter it down. Sir Eustace was

100

speaking again, but by now even he was starting to show signs of strain. "All right, Brand. Tell us just what you're getting at."

"That's better," said Brand. "I thought you would start to see sense before long. One thing I do have with me, fortunately, is a sharp knife. It was meant to be used for cutting rope, but it will do equally well for cutting throats—and unless you accept my terms, that is exactly what will happen. You can listen in if you like. Nagata first, I think, and then Fisher; I'll save young Lorrimer until the last. I don't imagine you will doubt that I mean what I say."

Sir Eustace breathed hard. "That won't help you."

Brand gave a short laugh. "Perhaps not; but as I remember telling one of your friends, Alpha has no time for failures. If I manage to escape from this cabin, my life will still be worth very little unless I can make amends. Oh, I admit that even I have no idea who is commander of Alpha, but I am a realist, as you will admit."

Vale banged against the door. "Well, then—come out, and take what's coming to you!"

"Not so fast," said Brand. "Even a realist must be allowed to have his dreams, and I still hold most of the cards. I will give you my terms, Wainwright. If you give me the small ferry, plus an hour's start before raising the alarm, your friends will be unharmed. If you refuse, I will cut their throats one by one. You'd better do some quick thinking."

"I see," said Sir Eustace softly. "I see. Very clever. I'm bound to admit—and very difficult." He raised his voice. "I will have to consider, Brand. I'll give you my answer in five minutes."

"No radio calls, then." Brand's voice was almost a snarl. "Remember, I am not bluffing!"

101

"I never thought you were, and in any case the radio in the control room is out of action," said Sir Eustace, and gestured quickly. "Back to the corridor —far enough to be out of earshot. Thor, stay right outside the door, and keep listening."

Scott winced as Juan Santos pulled him back. It was a devilish position; he could see no way out, and for once Sir Eustace seemed as baffled as the rest. "He'll do it, without a doubt," said Vale grimly. "After all, he's got nothing to lose. Anyone from Alpha will be given pretty short shrift."

"True, but there is something else which just might be of use," said Sir Eustace. "Brand's truth-drug, or whatever he calls it, may turn out to be a double-edged weapon. If we lay hands on him and inject him, he'll be bound to tell us everything he knows about Alpha, which would be the breakthrough we've been hunting for years. There's a faint chance that we might be able to call his bluff, rather than letting him call ours."

Scott broke in. "It won't work. Listen." he struggled up, flinching at the pain of his arm and head. "If he gets caught, he'll be cooped up in prison for years —perhaps even for the rest of his life. That'll happen anyway, so what has he got to lose by knifing Nigel and the others?"

There was a short silence. "He's right," said Vale slowly. "Sometimes I wonder whether we were wrong in doing away with hanging or shooting murderers . . . Try it, Eustace, but you'll have to make up your mind first."

"I've already done that," said Sir Eustace. "We'll talk, at least." He swung himself back toward the door, and rapped on it. "All right, Brand. Ready to listen?"

Brand replied promptly. "Go on."

"I'll give you my terms, then. Come out quietly, and I give you my promise that I will do my best for you, which is more than you deserve. Otherwise, you will be well and truly in the proverbial cart. Even the United Nations hasn't yet given up the death penalty for what it calls 'crimes against humanity', you know."

Brand laughed. "Talk sense, and don't be so stupid. I've told you that my life will be worth nothing unless I can make my own plans, and I could hardly do that from the inside of a prison cell. We've wasted enough time, Wainwright. It's your last chance. The ferry, and an hour's start—or else you can say good-bye to these three. Anything to say, Lorrimer?"

There was no reply, and Brand spoke again. "You gave me five minutes; now I give you twenty seconds. Yes or no?"

Sir Eustace drew a deep breath. "Much though I dislike the idea, I'm bound to admit that for the moment you hold the whip-hand. All right, Brand— you win. I accept."

CHAPTER 11

ESCAPE!

Brand's voice came through again, harsh and uncertain. "You understand, Wainwright? You swear that you will allow me to take the small ferry and blast away freely?"

"That's what I said," agreed Sir Eustace. "I'm afraid you'll have to trust my word, but that shouldn't be too difficult. Oddly enough I happen to be old-fashioned, and when I make a solemn promise I always keep it—even when it's made with a cowardly rat, if you'll forgive such a description of you. You're quite safe. Come out."

Scott held his breath. He could picture Brand's state of mind only too well. Once he unlocked the door he would be at their mercy, and if Sir Eustace chose to break his word there was nothing to stop him. Sir Eustace glanced across, and gave a slight smile. "I can guess what you're all thinking, but I imagine you will agree with me? The first thing is to get those three out, after we can go into conference. At least we won't have friend Brand bothering us."

"You mean to let him go, then?" muttered Voronov.

"Certainly I do. As I said, I'm old-fashioned, and that goes for Reggie too," said Sir Eustace, and tapped the door. "Hurry up, my dear fellow. I've told you that there's nothing to keep you."

Slowly the door swung open, and Brand lurched into the light of the corridor; his face was white, and in his hand he held an ugly-looking knife. Sir Eustace motioned him away. "Most unfriendly," he said. "I always said you were a nasty piece of work, and I've come to the conclusion that that is the understatement of the century. May I ask what you propose to do when you've said good-bye?"

Brand swung forward, and Santos stepped across into the cabin, followed by Voronov; Thor remained outside, watching Brand like a hawk, while Vale stood with his hand in his pocket, presumably holding a gun of some kind. "That will be my decision," said Brand. "You may have won this time, Wainwright, but you haven't seen the last of me!"

Sir Eustace sighed. "How very dramatic. 'A time will come, forsooth!' Well, I don't want to hurry you, but if you mean to go I think you'd better make a start. I am a mild-tempered person, as you know, but I admit that the urge to put my fist in your face is becoming really overwhelming, knife or no knife. Go on. We'll see you off. All right in there, Gregory?"

Voronov nodded, and stood back. "I'm fine," muttered Nigel; Scott managed to push forward, and gripped him by the shoulder. "I thought we were done for that time . . . Look after Ham—the brute cracked him on the head."

Fisher had come out of the cabin; Voronov was untying the still-senseless Nagata, and Sir Eustace pointed. "On your way, Brand," he said quietly. "Put that knife down. I needn't tell you that any one of us would welcome the excuse to hit you with a stunner."

It was only then that Scott fully realized that Sir Eustace really meant what he had said. "What about the others?" he asked suddenly. "Dupont and that swine Alec, I mean. They're still out cold."

Brand shrugged. "They were not in our agreement, and the ferry will hold only one," he said. "You are welcome to them, Wainwright. You needn't think that they will be able to tell you much about Alpha, even if you inject them with our special drug. Even I know very little about the organization as a whole, and they know nothing which will be of the slightest help to you. Try it if you don't believe me."

"I think we'll leave that until we've got them back home," snapped Vale. "Give me that knife before you put on your suit. I'll be coming through the airlock with you." He rammed his helmet into position, and waited; there was a long pause, and then Brand threw the knife to one side. "That's better. Keep listening, Eustace."

It was a strange situation; Scott watched, still wincing at each throb of his arm, and wondering whether Brand had some trick left even now. Then Brand drew on the suit that Thor was holding out, and both he and Vale checked their oxygen tanks and leads. Brand turned. "At least you keep your word," he said slowly. "I will be almost sorry when Alpha catches up with you. One hour, remember, and then you can do what you like."

Sir Eustace glanced at his watch, and nodded. The airlock door opened, and shut again as soon as Brand and Vale were inside the cramped compartment; the pressure-gauge began to swing, and they heard Vale's voice. "Vacuum. I'm opening up now."

Gregory Voronov came down the corridor, Nigel and Fisher by his side. "Is this wise? For all we know, he may have a lot more information than he makes out."

"He probably does, but unfortunately he forced us into a bargain which we must keep." Sir Eustace's tone was firm. "In precisely one hour we'll use the ferry radios to send out a general alert, and I don't honestly think that he can hope to get clear. Every radar scanner on Earth will be looking out for him, and he can't softly and silently vanish away, like the hunter of the Snark."

"That's what bothers me," muttered Scott. "He must have something up his sleeve!"

"That hadn't escaped me, but—oh, well, we'll have have to wait and see. Reggie! Answer, please."

"He's in the ferry," came Vale's voice in the head-phones. "Locks closed. Come out if you like."

"Why? I've no particular wish to wave him fare-well," said Sir Eustace. "In fact I'm extremely glad to see the last of him, at least for the moment. In any case, we ought to be able to see him from the observation window."

"Want a hand?" said Nigel softly, and Scott nodded. "That arm looks pretty rotten; you'll have to go and have it set. Boy, am I glad to see you!" He eased Scott along the corridor. "I'm darned if I remember much about it. When I came round I was back in that beastly cabin, and I couldn't see or hear a thing. I reckon it was about the nastiest time I've ever had."

"Just as nasty for us," said Scott soberly. "If we hadn't given in—oh, well, it's over now. There he goes."

The observation window gave a clear view of the docking port at the far end of Station Four, and as they watched they could see the smallest of the ferry-rockets start to glide away; there was a burst of power from its motor, and then the rocket shrank in size as it moved off. "Wonder what he'll try to do?" muttered Thor, pressing his face against the trans-parent window. "Somehow I don't like it."

"Nor do I, but it's better than we'd have dared to hope for a few minutes ago. Thor, I—well, I'm sorry." Nigel gave an embarrassed grin. "I thought you'd let us down."

Thor laughed. "I don't wonder. It was the only way to get a warning through, and I think it was about the only trick that Brand wouldn't have suspected. After all, there are not many people who can speak my language, and it was sheer luck that Reggie hap-pens to be one. French or German, or almost any-

107

thing else, would have been no good, but Icelandic is a different matter."

"Leave the talking until later," snapped Vale. "Mind you, I take my hat off to you, young Thor. It was a stroke of genius, and I'll have a lot to say about it when we have time, but at the moment we've other things to do. Check all the controls, and make sure that those other two beauties are tied up."

"I've already done that," said Voronov dryly. "I doubt whether they'll be pleased when they come round to find that Brand has left them here. How long, Eustace?"

"Fifty-five minutes precisely. That's odd," said Sir Eustace thoughtfully, peering through the observation window. "Unless I'm very much mistaken, he's deliberately put himself in the same orbit as our own. I'm not going crazy, am I?"

Vale thrust forward. "You're right. He must have done it deliberately. What's the game, I wonder?"

Sir Eustace shook his head. "I'm not ashamed to admit that I haven't the slightest idea. One thing we forgot to do was to check that ferry—yet another of our mistakes, though I don't see that it can have made much difference; he wouldn't have blasted off without knowing that there was plenty of fuel. But . . . well, there he is, and if he's still within range at the end of his hour's grace he'll have lost his last chance. Curiouser and curiouser."

Santos had gone back to see what could be done for Nagata, but the others stayed by the window, keeping their eyes fixed on the now small and star-like point that marked Brand's rocket. "I've no idea, at least," said Sir Eustace after a few minutes. "If anyone has a clue as to what's going on, it will be Dupont—or Alec; they're birds of a feather. I suggest that we do our best to bring them round, and see what they can tell us."

Scott shook himself, and gave a gasp of pain. "Look, can you give me a shot of something to numb this beastly arm? It feels as if it's on fire."

"My dear fellow, I'm sorry," said Sir Eustace quickly. I'm afraid we've been very selfish, but you must admit that the last quarter of an hour has been a little hectic. From what I can see, your arm isn't broken, but it's more than time we had a proper look at it."

Scott clenched his teeth as Nigel and Thor stripped off his jacket, washing his arm with disinfectant. Santos came in, looking satisfied. "Nagata will recover more quickly than I had thought," he said. "Stand back, please. I am a doctor, as you know, as well as a star-gazer, and I will ease the pain."

Scott shut his eyes, and winced as a needle sank into his arm. He almost fainted, but after a while the burning feeling started to wear off, and before long his arm was numb. Nigel and Thor stayed with him, while the others set to work making a thorough check of the rockets. "Better?" said Nigel quietly. "Phew! It's been quite a time."

"And it's not over yet," grunted Scott. "I don't trust the brute. Is he still there?"

"Yes, and he's only a few miles away. He's not moving," said Nigel. "Half an hour to go, and then we can get to work on him, as he'll know quite well. It beats me. Look, why don't we use the ferry radio to get a call back to Base?"

Thor shrugged. "I thought of that, but Reggie said it wouldn't help, and Eustace insists on leaving it for the full hour. I don't believe I could have been as straight as that. I'd have been tempted to stun Brand as soon as he came out."

"That's something my uncle would never do, Alpha or no Alpha," said Nigel. "All the same, I'm getting pretty edgy. It looks as if he's playing cat and mouse with us, not the other way round."

Still they waited, half-expecting something dramatic to happen. After another long pause Santos came in, this time pulling Dupont with him; the Frenchman was still unconscious, but his breathing was easier, and his face had started to lose its chalky whiteness. "He will come round soon," said Santos. "A few minutes, I think."

In fact it was a full quarter of an hour before Dupont's eyes flickered open. By then the checking had been finished, and the whole party had collected in the control room. Alec was still senseless, and Vale gave him a contemptuous glance. "We haven't bothered about him," he said in reply to Scott's unspoken question. "I wouldn't waste any dope on him, because he's not likely to know anything that Dupont doesn't. Dupont! Do you hear me?"

Dupont choked, and spoke in a slurred voice. "I—I do not understand. What has happened?"

"You've lost the game," said Vale grimly. "I wouldn't like to be in your shoes when you're handed over to security. Are you going to tell us all you know, or do I have to give you a jab of your own dope?"

Dupont writhed. "I—where is Brand? What do you mean?"

"Let me explain," said Sir Eustace calmly. "No point in bellowing at him, Reggie; you really do rush at things like the proverbial bull at a gate. This is the situation, my dear Dupont. We know most of the story, and you'll observe that your young friend is trussed up like a turkey. Unfortunately Brand forced us to let him go, and at the moment he's wandering outside in his ferry, which doesn't make sense to me. Talk!"

Dupont tried to struggle up. "Brand! He has gone?"

"Not very far," said Sir Eustace. "That's what is bothering me more than a little. I may as well be frank with you. There's something here which neither I nor the rest of us can fathom, and it'll be in your own interest to 'come clean', as they say in the old-fashioned gangster movies. Just what is Brand up to?"

Dupont's mouth opened, and for a few seconds he seemed unable to speak. "Brand! He has taken our ferry?"

"I certainly wasn't going to hand him one of ours," said Sir Eustace, with a hint of impatience. "Well?"

"You fool!" Dupont's voice rose to a scream. "How long has he been gone?"

Sir Eustace consulted his watch. "Exactly fifty-one minutes. We promised him an hour's start, and there isn't much of it left. After that, we can start the hunt."

Dupont's eyes rolled. "You will have no time," he said in a hoarse croak. "The ferry! In it there are weapons—deadly weapons. When Brand has prepared them, he will attack. The Station will be destroyed, and we will be destroyed with it. We are dead men!"

CHAPTER 12

BATTLE IN SPACE

Vale swung round and gripped Dupont by the shoulder, shaking him violently. "What the blazes do you mean? If you're trying some trick——"

"He is much too frightened," broke in Santos, pushing forward and staring into Dupont's face. "He is in the sweat, my friend. Please to explain."

Dupont was indeed sweating. "We have made missiles," he said in a stifled voice. "They are of new design, and of terrible power, even though they are small. If we do not leave this Station before he can make his missiles ready, we have no hope!"

"Don't talk rubbish," roared Vale. "He'd have no reason to blow the lot of us out of the sky, particularly with you and Kerry on board—no, wait. I start to see what you mean."

Sir Eustace was already half-way to the main door. "I think we'll make a move, if you don't mind," he said. "A ferry won't be so easy to hit as a Station. Load Dupont and Kerry into the second one—I suppose we'll have to take them with us, though I could do without the pleasure of their company."

The next minutes were frantic, particularly as there were four passengers; Alec and Nagata were unconscious, Dupont tied up and Scott more or less helpless, though he did his best. There were only three ferries in action, and there was no room to spare. Scott was half-pushed into the largest of the miniature rocket-ships, together with Vale, Nigel and Dupont, but it all took time, and every moment Scott expected to feel the shudder of an explosion. "What are they?" he muttered, as Vale switched on the motors. "Bombs? Sounds antique, but nasty enough if he scores a bull's-eye."

"Antique?" Dupont gave a short laugh. "But no. These missiles are guided, you understand. They will—what is the word?—home on to their target, and each one carries a nuclear explosive that will make your gunpowder bombs seem like little matches. Brand has himself designed them."

The ferry was drawing away from the Station now, and through the observation window Scott could see that the other rockets were ready to move; Sir Eustace and Voronov were on the first, together with Alec Kerry and Nagata, leaving Thor and Santos in the second. "You've a lot to explain," said Vale grimly. "Not much honour among villains, is there? If I'm thinking along the right lines, your friend Brand is anxious to wipe us out partly for revenge, and partly because he doesn't want you and Kerry to give away what you know. Correct?"

Dupont set his lips. "Those are the rules of our organization. There can be no failures."

"You've had one this time," said Nigel, and snorted contemptuously. "Look, there he is. That's old Brand, prancing about as if he owned the whole of space. He can't be more than a few miles off, Reggie. Why don't we go after him?"

"Talk sense," said Vale impatiently. "Putting a boarding-party on to a rocket may sound fine in the story-books, but I'd be most interested to hear just how you propose to do it. Also, I admit that I don't like the sound of those weapons we've been hearing about, and I know that Brand is a pretty good nuclear physicist—we even worked together for a time, many years ago. Get on to the radio, Nigel, and call up Eustace."

Nigel was already at the radio panel, and in a few seconds Sir Eustace's voice came through. "Well, at least we're out of the danger-zone, if there really is trouble ahead. Come in, please, Thor."

"Reading you," said Thor briefly. "Instructions, please."

"I wish I knew what instructions to give. This whole situation is ridiculous," said Sir Eustace. "Four ferry-rockets, floating about as if we were all getting ready to play bumper-cars. I can just imagine what the Sunday papers would make of it. What annoys me is that at the moment we can't get through to Station One."

"If——" began Vale, and then broke off as another voice came through the receiver. It was a voice that they all recognized, and Scott tensed, inwardly cursing the injured arm which put him so completely out of action. "Brand," he breathed. "Phew! the brute's got cheek, anyway!"

"Quiet," snapped Vale. "All right, Brand; we're receiving you. You'd better dock, and I'll promise you won't be hurt—not by us, at any rate," he added less loudly. "You can't get away."

"I'll waste no time on you," said Brand, as coldly as ever. "Whatever happens to me, I'm going to enjoy the next few minutes. You know about my new missiles?"

There was no reply; Scott wondered what Sir Eustace was thinking. Then Brand spoke again. "Very well; if you don't want to speak, you can listen.

114

I have four missiles, and all are ready for launching. Watch Station Four, Wainwright—and if you doubt me, go back there!"

"Do not go!" Scott had almost forgotten Dupont, but the Frenchman suddenly let out a cry. "It is no bluff, Vale. Keep away."

The radio crackled, and they heard Gregory Voronov. "Kerry has come round, and he's told us the same story as Dupont. It is true, I believe, but Brand may not be ready——"

"You fool!" rasped Brand; Scott could picture him, crouched in his ferry-rocket and bent on nothing but revenge. "Look, then. In less than five minutes Station Four will be destroyed, and that is only the beginning."

Nigel suddenly switched off the transmitter, and turned to Vale. "It doesn't sound like a stunt, Reggie. If he's right—well, he's got another three bangers left, one for each of us. What's the form? Run for it?"

"Keep the radio on," said Vale harshly, and waited until Nigel had tuned in again. "Eustace. Get back to Station One—you too, Gregory. We're staying out here."

Scott felt bewildered. It sounded like straight suicide, but Sir Eustace's reply was immediate. "Received and understood. We will return to Station One as quickly as possible. Acknowledge, Thor."

"Understood," said Thor, his voice distorted through the ever-increasing hiss of the receiver. "Keep calling."

Nigel and Scott stared at each other, but neither felt inclined to say anything, and there was a long silence, broken only by the radio hiss which sounded like an angry snake. Vale gave a brief burst from the motors, and swung the ferry round until Station Four was in full view. "If I'm right, Brand is just about to place his ace. We can't stop him, and all we can do is to watch and see just what effect it has . . . Look there. Can you see it?"

"What?"

"There—coming from about ninety degrees. He wasn't bluffing. Watch out."

Scott eased himself painfully up to the observation window, and strained his eyes. Now he could see something new; it was a luminous patch, and it was moving toward the Station with apparent slowness. "Missile," breathed Nigel, close beside him. "He's bound to miss from that range. It isn't like taking a pot-shot at a clay pigeon!"

"You heard what Dupont said. It's a 'homer', so it will go straight to its target," muttered Vale. "Confound it, I left some valuable papers on board the Station. I don't give much for their chances now."

It was a strange moment. Scott, Nigel and Vale watched as though hypnotized as the shining patch crept closer and closer to the great space station which showed up as a dark mass against the background of stars; they were on the night-side of the Earth, and to all appearances they might have been alone in the universe. Now the patch was almost up to its target, and Scott pressd his face hard against the window. "I don't believe it'll work," he half-whispered. "The thing's a dud!"

Then, suddenly, there was a flash which almost blinded him, and made him pull back from the window with a shout of pain. The hiss from the radio rose to a roar, and Scott almost fancied that he could feel a jolt, though he knew subconsciously that he was letting his imagination get the better of him. "It's not a dud,"

116

muttered Nigel in an awestruck voice. "Reggie, look. Just look at that!"

Station Four was no longer graceful and symmetrical. As the brilliant light died away they could see that the whole Station was distorted; it was spinning crazily around, and it was no longer in one piece. It was hard to make out just what had happened, but Scott realized that one of the main arms had broken clear and was drifting away. Then came another explosion, this time from inside the main body of the Station; another, and another, and another, until nothing but twisted wreckage remained of what had been one of mankind's greatest achievements. "It's gone," said Scott stupidly. "Nigel, it's gone. It can't be true!"

"Did you doubt it? I told you that you were fools." Dupont had struggled half-up, despite his ropes, and was staring at them almost triumphantly. "Alpha does not fail. You have ruined much of the work we have done over the years, but you will pay the price. Station One is next."

Scott gave a shout. "No!"

"He'll try it," said Vale curtly, his hand on the switch of the radio; the hiss died away as he turned the control. "That should be interesting, particularly as we'll have a ringside seat. I wouldn't chatter away, Dupont. If I hear another word, I won't be able to stop myself from clouting you. Be warned."

"But—but for Pete's sake, there are people on our Station!" said Nigel hysterically. "If he can—well, do the same thing, they won't stand a chance, and there aren't enough ferries to get everyone off in time!"

"The point hadn't escaped me," said Vale, still in the same curt, steady tone. "Keep Brand in sight if

117

you can. He's no faster than we are, and I'm giving full power."

Scott was shaking. "You take it darned calmly," he breathed. "There must be something we can do!"

Nigel broke in. "If you had your screen ready, it would stop him, but you told me yourself that it wouldn't be ready for a test until the end of the year— and Brand got that out of me when I was doped. Can't we ram him, or something?"

Still Vale said nothing, and both Scott and Nigel felt helpless as well as horribly puzzled. Brand's rocket was still in view, but there was no sign of the other two ferries, and Nigel clutched Scott's shoulder. "They'll be back in One by now. That means they'll go up in smoke too. Reggie, what's going to happen?"

"Watch, and you'll see—at least, I think so," said Vale, and brought the motors into action again; but now Station One was in view, half-illuminated by the sun so that its main cylinder and two of the arms shone out brightly. "You can haul Dupont up to the far window, if you like. I want him to see this one too."

Then, at last, Scott began to understand; but there was no time to ask questions, and he watched as Nigel grabbed Dupont and pushed him over to the window. "Can't we call up?" muttered Nigel. "I can't stand this. Some of them will be able to get away——"

"You won't be able to get through," said Vale brusquely. "For the moment we're out of touch with Station One. Try, if you like, but you won't have any luck, and neither will Brand, for that matter. There they go—two of them!"

Once again Scott strained his eyes; once again he could see two sinister patches of light, both crawling

118

toward the Station. He had lost sight of Brand's ferry, but presumably it was somewhere out there, hidden because its dark side was turned toward them. "We can't stop them," said Nigel in a dull, hopeless whisper. I can't look!"

"Keep watching," rapped Vale. "Two minutes, I reckon."

It was the longest two minutes of Scott's life; Nigel had turned away, breathing in short gasps. "Any moment now," said Vale, still in the same calm tone. "Yes. There it goes!"

Scott leaped back to the window, Nigel by his side. Dupont said something, but his words were drowned by a triumphant roar from Vale. "You see? No damage; there can't be." He broke into a laugh. "A perfect case of an ace being well and truly trumped. Now do you understand?"

"I—I don't," said Nigel blankly. "I don't get it. I saw the things bang off, but the Station's still there——"

"Of course it is," said Vale, and pointed. "What you can't see, you idiot, is my screen. It's all round Station One; the transmitters were switched on at full blast—Eustace saw to that, believe me—and any explosive, nuclear or otherwise, will be triggered off long before it's close enough to do any harm." He turned away from the window. "You ought to have trusted me better than that. Do you seriously think I'd have been sitting here, doing nothing, if I thought the Station might be in any real danger?"

"Sorry," muttered Nigel. "I still don't get it, though. You told me the screen wouldn't be ready for months yet, and that's what Brand got out of me."

Vale gave a mirthless grin. "I'm afraid we weren't one hundred per cent honest with you, but it was in a

119

good cause." He gave a burst of power, and turned the ferry until it was facing away from the Station. "The screen was finished some time back, and we'd done so many tests that I was absolutely sure of its effectiveness. On the other hand, the last thing we wanted was for Alpha to know, so to be on the safe side I fed you with wrong information just in case you ran into trouble on Four—as you certainly did. Once you were doped, you had to tell the truth as you knew it. Luckily, it wasn't true at all."

"I see," said Nigel slowly, and managed a grin in return. "Rotten trick, Reggie, but I suppose it was the right thing to do." He paused. "Is that why you couldn't call up Station One by radio?"

Vale nodded. "Of course. One of the unfortunate effects of the screen is that it blocks out wireless waves as well as everything else, and once the transmitters are switched on there's complete radio cut-off, which is something I'll have to try to alter in the near future. Can you see Brand's ferry anywhere? I doubt if he's feeling very pleased with life just at the moment."

"He must be hopping mad," said Scott. "Phew! I feel as limp as a wet rag. Wonder what he'll do? Run for it?"

"Probably, but he won't get far." Vale peered through the observation window. "The trouble is that if Dupont is right, he's got one missile left, and that means that we can't afford to switch off the screen. He may try for one of the other Stations. I hope he does, because I needn't add that they have full protection as well. So have we, so there's no need to start getting jumpy."

"You mean that this ferry's fitted up, too?"

"I wouldn't have risked staying out here otherwise," said Vale dryly. "If Brand had the chance, he'd blow
120

us out of the Solar System and enjoy it. In fact, I believe he's going to try. Look there!"

"It's another of them," muttered Scott. "Is it making for us?"

Vale moved quickly over to the main control panel, and pulled a lever. There was a low humming noise, and Scott fancied that he could feel a slight tingle running through his body. "I won't try to explain just how it works," said Vale, "but I assure you that it'll do the trick. The bang will happen when the bomb, or whatever you call it, is a full three miles away, which is much too far to do us any damage at all. On the whole, I'm rather glad. It's pleasing to have a bird's-eye view, and I don't expect I'll ever have another chance."

The missile was becoming brighter now, and Scott stared at it. But for the invisible screen all round them, that innocent-looking spark of light would destroy them in the fraction of a second. He was no longer frightened; his faith in Vale was complete, but all the same it was an eerie sensation.

Then, suddenly, he felt a violent blow, and he lurched sideways, crying out as a fresh jab of pain shot through his arm. Vale spun round, but he was too late. Dupont was free; somehow or other he had managed to wriggle out of his ropes, and in his hand he held a massive metal box that had been lying on the floor. Before any of the three could stop him, the box had smashed into the main panel. There was a flash, a high-pitched whine, and the humming stopped; the lights inside the ferry went out, plunging the cabin into semi-darkness, and Vale shouted desperately. "Get him, Nigel! Screen's out of action—get him, I say! Quick!"

121

CHAPTER 13

THE LAST THROW

Nigel threw himself across the cabin, and lashed out. His fist smashed against Dupont's jaw, and the Frenchman gave a cry; then he went limp, and Nigel hit him again. "Rope, Scott. I'll truss him so that he won't get out in a hundred years. What's the damage?"

Vale was working furiously at the control panel. "Bad enough," he said harshly. "Hold on." The spacecraft accelerated, pressing Scott hard against the far wall of the cabin. "Watch that light. If it catches up with us, we're finished!"

Scott hauled himself back to the observation window. "It's coming in. I don't reckon we'll beat it to the Station."

Vale gave a quick look. "You're right. Nigel, handle the motors, and keep as clear as you can; we can't get inside the Station screen before it catches us. I'll have to get the transmitter working somehow or other. The damage isn't really serious, but ordinarily it would take half an hour to fix, and we've only got a few minutes. Full power, Nigel!"

Nigel needed no urging; the motors roared, but still the threatening light came closer and closer, growing more brilliant every second. "How far?" rapped Vale. "Make a guess, if you can."

"A mile, I'd say," breathed Scott. "Alter course, and we may be able to dodge it."

Nigel obeyed; again there was a momentary feeling of weight as the ferry changed direction, and Scott thought that the manœuvre had succeeded, but then he saw to his horror that the light was still brightening. "It's homing in on us, all right," he said. His mouth felt clammy, and he could not hide the fact that he was almost as scared as he had been during that nightmare time in the airlock. "No chance of shooting it down?"

"What with? We're unarmed," snapped Vale. "Confound it, I can't get the screen working without going into dock. Head for the Station, Nigel—curve round as much as you can. It's our only chance!"

Nigel gritted his teeth, and altered the angle of the rocket jet yet again. "It'll take us five minutes at least. What's the range?"

"About three miles, so far as I can tell. You'll have to risk crashing into the Station," said Vale steadily. "You're our best pilot, young Nigel, so we'll leave it to you; we've got to get well inside the screen before we're hit. Try a call on the radio, Scott. There's a chance that the Station screen has been switched off, I suppose, and we've no other way of telling."

Scott pulled himself together, and swung across to the radio. Then he turned round. "No good; the set's smashed well and truly. Shall I have a tinker with it?"

"No point," said Vale, staring through the window. "I'm sorry, both of you; I ought to have had more sense, but I couldn't foresee this. If we go up in smoke we'll take that swine Dupont with us, but that's not much comfort. How far now?"

Scott was by his side. Ahead, still a frightening distance away, he could see the outline of the Station, but the gleaming light was coming in from the side

123

as though trying to intercept them. It was no longer a point, but a small disk. "We're running short of fuel," breathed Nigel. "I've been using all our reserves, and there's only a couple of minutes' supply left."

"It may be enough," said Vale; even at that moment Scott felt a surge of admiration at his coolness. "Keep going as long as you can."

Scott knew that he was helpless; there was nothing that any of them could do—except hope. He listened to the steady roar of the rocket motor, knowing that the slightest falter would mean death, and he tried not to think about what would happen if they lost the race. "Get ready," said Vale at last. "We'll be hit in less than a minute now, I think, so you'll have to head straight for the Station and trust to luck."

It was a desperate moment. The missile was very near, and as it closed in it grew ominously in size; but the Station was near too, apparently rushing toward them. Scott wanted to scream. "Will we know when we're inside the barrier?" he muttered. "I mean, will we feel anything?"

Vale shook his head. "Not a chance. It's touch and go all right; I reckon we've about half a minute yet."

Suddenly the steady note of the motor faltered, and Nigel gave a shout. "Fuel," he said, his face pale. "We're out—we can't accelerate. This is it, Reggie!"

The missile seemed to veer off course. It was no longer making straight for them, and Vale pointed. "Quick! We're inside, but it may be too late. Put your suits on in case we're holed!"

Scott reached for his helmet, but before he could reach it there came a blinding flash; the missile flickered, and there was a jolt as the ferry shuddered.

124

"Like being hit with a hammer," thought Scott, and he shut his eyes, expecting every second that the rocket would be cracked open like an eggshell. Lurch —jolt! He heard Vale call out, and then, slowly, the shuddering died away. The missile had gone, and the sense of relief made him dizzy. "We'll overshoot the Station," said Nigel hoarsely. "We can't pull up, but I reckon they'll have seen us."

Vale rammed his spectacles back on to his nose, and stared through the window at the now-empty blackness of space. "They'll have seen us, all right, and they'll guess what happened," he said quietly. "It's over, thank Heaven. We've enough oxygen to last us until we can be picked up, and we're in a safe orbit. Well done, both of you. We'll never be closer to death than we were less than a minute ago."

Commander Richard Thomson lay back on his couch, and looked around him. The control room in Station One was crowded; all the scientists were there, together with Scott, Nigel and Thor, while Sir Eustace beamed at them in the manner of a friendly headmaster. "I think we can tidy up the loose ends soon enough," said Thomson. "The miracle is that we seem to have come through without any casualties at all, though I can't understand how! How about your head, Ham?"

Hamilton Fisher smiled ruefully. "It aches, but that's nothing to fret about," he said. "Kaz Nagata is on the mend, but I reckon it'll be weeks before he's one hundred per cent; he had a pretty rough time. Even now I don't know the full story of how you got wise to us."

Vale pointed to the three boys. "Those are the lads you've got to thank," he said. "I'm not sure we were right in sending them on what turned out to be a trip into a very nasty lion's den, but they pulled it off in no uncertain manner. That bit of Icelandic was sheer genius, young Thor!"

"I couldn't think of anything else," said Thor calmly. "The worst of it was that I had to play the coward, and I didn't like it one bit."

Nigel flushed. "I've said I'm sorry. Crikey, what else could I think? No, I ought to have known better," he said. "I'm a nitwit, I suppose."

"Not really. You couldn't tell," said Thomson. "Well, I don't propose to hand out any special compliments. We've won this round, but don't think we've heard the last of Alpha. Dupont and Kerry are out of harm's way, and they won't be able to do any more damage, but there's still Brand, and plenty of others as well. There's a lot that we still don't know."

"Brand," echoed Scott. "What's the latest? Remember, I've been out of action having my arm done up—and boy, is it still sore! Did he get away after all?"

"He did, I regret to tell you," said Sir Eustace placidly. "He must have known that his delightful little plan had misfired, but where he went after that is anybody's guess. He simply melted away into thin air—or, rather, thin space. Unfortunately we couldn't chase him, because we couldn't get any radio messages through until we'd got the screen turned off, which took some time. He's as slippery as a whole bucketful of eels, and a great deal more slimy. I'd like to have a serious talk with him."

Thomson shrugged. "Wouldn't we all? Mind you, I don't for one moment think that he's the top man,

126

and he was probably telling the truth when he said that even he didn't know who was really running Alpha. Well, Brand can wait, and at least he won't have another chance to take us in."

"That strikes a raw note," admitted Sir Eustace. "I was never happy about Brand—or Dupont either, for that matter—but Alec Kerry was a different matter, and I'm ashamed to say that he hoodwinked me completely. I suppose we all make mistakes, and that was a bad one." He turned to Scott and Thor. "All the same, I don't imagine than we are in any doubt about our other new recruits. You've had quite a hectic beginning to your career as an astronaut, young Scott. If you want to say 'good-bye' and go back to a nice, quiet job in a bank, or something equally worthy, I won't argue. What do you say?"

"Need you ask?" said Scott slowly. "I'm here, and this is where I'm going to stay. Just you try to stop me!" He stared through the observation window; below he could see the lights of Earth, but they seemed very far away. "I belong to space now, just as much as the rest of you."

"I thought as much," murmured Sir Eustace. "I don't think you'll regret it."

Armada Science Fiction

Step into the strange world of Tomorrow with Armada's
exciting science fiction series.

ARMADA SCI-FI 1
ARMADA SCI-FI 2
ARMADA SCI-FI 3

Edited by Richard Davis

**Three spinechilling collections of thrilling tales of fantasy
and adventure, specially written for Armada readers.**

Read about . . . The monstrous Aliens at the bottom of
the garden . . . A jungle planet inhabited by huge
jellies . . . A robot with a human heart . . . The terrible,
terrifying Trodes . . . A mad scientist and his captive
space creatures . . . The deadly rainbow stones of
Lapida . . . The last tyrannosaur on earth . . . and many
more.
Stories to thrill you, stories to amuse you—and stories to
give you those sneaking shivers of doubt . .

Begin your sci-fi library soon!

Armada